SAVED

SAVED

The re-booting of humanity
and the planet

Suzy Blake

SAVED
THE RE-BOOTING OF HUMANITY AND THE PLANET

iUniverse books may be ordered through booksellers or by contacting:

iUniverse
1663 Liberty Drive
Bloomington, IN 47403
www.iuniverse.com
844-349-9409

ISBN: 978-1-6632-3052-2 (sc)
ISBN: 978-1-6632-3053-9 (e)

Library of Congress Control Number: 2022907530

Print information available on the last page.

iUniverse rev. date: 06/20/2022

This book is dedicated to my most favorite loves, Jim, Garrett, Gretchen, Courtney and Zippy.

ACKNOWLEDGMENTS

There are so many people who have helped me shape this book, some I know personally, others I have met through their own books. I do believe everyone you meet in life is a teacher. I am overwhelmed by the generosity and love I've received. I could not have written this without you, my teachers.

To Jim Grossklas, who read every word of this manuscript a hundred times, who helped me immeasurably with all the computer stuff that I have an aversion to, who made sure I remembered to eat, to take breaks and who rubbed my neck after hours typing.

To Mike Grossklas, who read this as it progressed and encouraged me throughout the process of this creation, who thanked me for entertaining him with this book.

To Hannah Bellaf, my dear friend, who read the first draft of this book and continued to cheer me on writing even though it meant I had no time to go to lunch with her.

To Theresa Fieberts, my joy-filled spiritual leader at the Center for Spiritual Living who helped me remember this dream by meditating and cheered me on.

To all the other teachers who I met through their writings, Wayne Dyer, Marianne Williamson, Neal Donald Walsh, Ernest Holmes, Raine Eisler, Erick von Daniken, Philip Coppens, Mark Hawkins, Joe Dispenza, Dan Millman, Ram Dass, Michael Beckwith, Bruce Lipton, and countless others. Thank you for your words, your insights, your lessons and your experiences.

Again, to my son Garrett and his wife Gretchen who read the first draft and made a suggestion that turned my skeleton of a story into a whole-body book. THANK YOU!

The future belongs to those
who believe in the beauty of their dreams.

Eleanor Roosevelt

DAY ONE

Logan Cieslak planned to leave work early for a dentist appointment. He never made it.

Intense white light was everywhere, as if the planet were getting its picture taken from some other planet. Hundreds of planes full of people that circle the globe on their collective journeys were being handled by the light. Immediately they were all safe on the ground at the destination airports.

At this time the space pods, disks of a silver material, were becoming visible as they descended from the light. The smooth surface revealed no evidence of doors or windows, and each pod was approximately fifty yards in diameter. The silver pods were spaced out in a mile-apart grid covering the globe. Before too much panic ensued, a voice was heard. It was a deep voice, yet soft and kind. It was heard on every form of media as well as outdoors. It was intended for all humans on the planet to hear the messages.

"We come in peace and love. Do not bother to activate your military. You do not possess anything that could even remotely faze us.

"We come from the God Center in peace and love. We put you here. We gave you this planet quite some time ago and we have been watching you, all of you everywhere, surprise and disappoint us. Yes, we are now broadcasting from all of your media and have taken over communications, just temporarily. We are broadcasting in every one of the six thousand languages simultaneously so that everyone on this planet can hear us and understand why we are here and what we are doing.

"For those of you awaiting a Second Coming, be it Christ, Messiah, or whoever your religion says is coming to save you someday, this my children, is The Day. We are here to save humanity and the planet from destruction. We come from the God Center, the creator of all and everything. There is no need to panic. We will communicate all that needs to be done and we will be here to see that it is complete.

"We are going to be speaking like this to the entire planet for about 30 minutes a day to everyone, giving you educational information and purposes to retrain all of you. We will speak to all governments to restructure them. All of your military weaponry has been deactivated. You cannot kill your Creator."

There was, of course, panic at the White House where a silver pod was hovering. The president went out to the balcony, his aides having given him a bullhorn for communicating. "Who is your leader?" he demanded, with his staff hovering behind him. The bullhorn, totally over-done in terms of communication, is amusing the God Center who hears every word, and knows what is in each heart, including what people are thinking.

"We have much to tell all of you but for the USA, let's just start with you. The God Center could not fathom how you came to lead this country and that does not speak well for those who voted for you. Your government is such a mess that we have chosen to rebuild it. You may not like it if you are in government, but it is beyond the time that any one person could affect enough change to get things right. There is majesty in this moment of your history."

"Shoot them down! I want them destroyed!" the president screamed as his staff was trying to guide him off of the balcony and back into the Oval Office, now packed with people.

"Save it," the voice shot back. "I told you already your weaponry is not capable of making so much as a tiny dent in our fleet. Everyone needs to calm down and listen. We are in charge of this planet. We put you here to develop and evolve. My children, you once had passion, good intentions, curiosity and a love of nature. There was a time when we smiled down at you on Earth because you were accomplishing great things. You all are children of the God Center. You were not created to kill each other, or profit from making people sick. We've heard so many cry out to us to make things right and we will.

"We watched as the love of money and power took over. We watched as the Earth was abused, ravaged for trinkets like diamonds, pounded for oil and polluted like a garbage dump.

"We have come now to reconstruct, rebuild and reboot humanity and the planet. We are like a super conductor launching each individual instrument into a collective sound. This planet is an unimaginably huge orchestra. We also have to teach some in this orchestra how to play the instrument you are! You had the capability to fix things yourselves, and while some good people tried, they could not overcome the greed-and-power people. You who operate on power and greed will be in for a major adjustment.

"You have had many 'visitors' on this planet. Did you ever stop to ask yourselves how there are so many different versions, or races, of humans on this planet? How have you reconciled this? Five major races are on one planet. Have you ever wondered how this happened?

"The God Center has populated many planets with a variety of humans and some human-likes. For your information, there are entire planets of black skinned people, other planets are Oriental, every race of people you have here, come from their own planet. On Earth we wanted to combine many of our creations, hoping you would all get along and realize you are one. Sadly, this has not happened. Racial differences are problematical, but you are created equally and with great love, all of you! You have such a ridiculous fear of 'aliens' not even realizing you all are. And to think Earthlings have wondered if there was life 'out there'. Yes. Yes, there is.

"You have had resident 'visitors' teaching physics and engineering thousands of Earth years ago. Do you know who this was? Many Earthlings called them Sky Gods. The God Center sent them to you from other planets we created, and they are extremely advanced.

"You should be too, not that we want to shame you. But you need to clearly see that the way you have progressed is self-destructive. We have come to show you how the other planets have made their progress. We have come to reveal secrets that have been hidden for centuries to keep power away from you, to manipulate you. We have come to help advance your Earths technology and to greatly improve your health. So do not fear this intervention. Without it you will all perish."

People everywhere were speechlessly glued to media sources listening on televisions, computers, phones, and radios. It wasn't necessary to be within range of any media source since the voice could be heard outside and inside every dwelling.

There were collective shudders for some, tears for others. Tech centers had people scrambling to take back control over the broadcasting to no avail, while at the Pentagon a major defensive scramble could not take place because the silver pods had the power to control all aircraft, missiles, and all communicating devices.

"You control nothing, so please stop trying. We ask that you listen. Try to wrap your heads around the fact that this is a global message, a global do-over. We want to give you all a chance for a good productive life. You cannot fight this. Anyone who is not willing to listen and then to cooperate will be removed from the planet. The common cry the God Center has heard is that everyone wants peace on Earth. We are here to make that happen."

"You cannot hold this country hostage! You cannot hold me hostage! Who are you? I want to speak to a person!" screamed the president back on the balcony with his bullhorn, waving his arms at the pod above him

4

while dripping with sweat. He had refused to go to an undisclosed safe room believing he could control everything.

"Would you like to be the first removed? We so nearly did remove you, several times in fact. But we come from love and peace. We are not 'persons' like human beings. We have no form, though we can take any material form we chose. We are energy and you must get over the fact that humans are just humans and you do not rule the entire universe. We do. We made you, as we keep telling you. We want everyone everywhere to have a good life and we are here to make that happen. You control absolutely nothing right now. The absolute hubris on this planet! You think you are all that matters yet your archaeologists and scientists deny the truth about your history. We will make truth your fuel for going forward."

"We have a lot of work to do. Assemble your government representatives – all of them, to their respective halls – now. You can all hear me so go get in your places please."

"What about me? What about your president?"

"You are certainly not our president. The fact that you are president of anything other than the Liars Club or the Egomaniacs Club is beyond all understanding. The president, according to your own government creation serves at the will of the people. All the government people serve, or at least that is what you are currently telling yourselves. In fact, you are all more about money and power, talking your way into endorsements from corporate donors. You want to protect the perks you enjoy that the average person only dreams about, while tending to your multiple homes. You violate your own oaths to serve the people by enriching yourselves at the people's expense. We are going to be making some very big changes."

People working in the offices of the National Intelligence Department headed immediately to the conference room, switching on the wall of television screens. The Department of Defense sent representatives scurrying to the meeting. Logan joined up with Jessie Ulbrich and Manuel Tima, the trio being the department's UAP (Unidentified Aerial Phenomena) research team.

"I think we are about to find out why they've been watching us," Logan whispered to them.

"What the hell? Look at the TV monitors! Every one of them shows the Earth enclosed in a grid of silver dots!" Manuel exclaimed. "But think about this! The pictures are from space, not Earth."

As people flooded the room all eyes were focused on the screens with nearly perfect silence, save for a few gasps of Oh My God! Listening to the voice, some taking notes, some starring open mouthed in shocking disbelief of what they were seeing.

"We're being invaded – get the missiles ready!" shouted the Director.

"No, it is NOT an attack! Listen! It's the God Center and besides the sheer amount of these silver discs makes us pathetically inadequate to attack them." Logan countered.

"Director, we have studied UAP activity for decades. We have seen these discs before, many times, just not in this number. We have been watched and studied. Now let's listen to this voice that says its bringing peace to Earth."

The senators and congressional representatives were assembling in their great halls, all of them holding their phones to listen as they gathered. Their faces are showing mixtures of fear and curiosity, some visibly shaking as they take their places in the elegant governmental chambers.

The God Center continued.

"Your cooperation is appreciated. We have a lot to do. We are working with governments worldwide. You will only hear what pertains to your country for now. We have much work to do with all the governments worldwide. We are changing all of them radically. Here is the plan for the U.S.

"By your own creating, there are 100 senators, 532 people in congress, and 435 representatives. You are not all here, we see, but here's the thing people. Since we know everything, including everything in your hearts, and minds, we must say this group of people assembling here is one collective sewer of intentions, wow. Here are the rules for your new improved government going forward.

"Number One - Your terms are up one year from today. In the future, there is a four-year limit on all positions – all positions, even state and local areas so I hope everyone is paying attention. The intention is to have one day, every four years, where everyone votes for everything. It will be a holiday so all can vote without complications.

"Number Two - You serve the people, not yourselves. No monetary endorsements or contributions from corporations will be allowed. We don't know how in the Earth realm you blew this so badly, but folks, this lobbying thing, this corporations being people? No way. Get serious.

"Number Three - Your salaries are so overinflated – let's hear it for greed – and that too will end. You will make three hundred dollars per week, when you are working in Washington only. You think we're kidding? No. No we are not. If you want to make more money than that, you are not working for the people so get out of government. You will be given housing so that your presence in Washington is full time because people, you work here.

"This is a good start. So, who is in? Anyone want to walk out right now? You can. You can just walk out and go home. There is no negotiating anything. We know there are a handful of really good people in this group. Sadly, it is not the majority. We have much work to do in terms of cleaning up your government. It will be a process."

For decades the polarization of the two-party system were at odds with each other. People grew angry. It seemed they were being ignored while their government officials played power games. Now they all faced the same transformation. Dictators in other countries responded in a similar fashion.

"Is anyone rethinking their career choice? You are all now dismissed to either go to your respective offices to take notes on what the new rules are or to pack it up. Your choice. You were given free will at birth, you know. We thought that was really a good idea. It's been pretty messed up through the ages."

"We hear all of you everywhere, trying to figure out if this is an alien invasion, and we hear those of you plotting how to come out of this on top, and we hear the intellectually challenged creating conspiracy nonsense. We had no idea there were so many comedians among you. The markets and banks have been temporarily suspended, frozen in other words. This is so those of you who would try to do some massive moving of money are prohibited from doing so. This is for the common good, something you desperately need to focus on from now on."

People were listening. There was a stampede for bars and churches. Being with other people, while listening to the broadcast seemed to bring a sense of safety in numbers. With so many congregating together it was eerily quiet as they focused on the broadcast.

A loud cheer went up when the God Center spoke of the new rules for government. For many years the people had been angry at the politicians for being more concerned about their donors than the people they were supposed to represent. The politicians all made promises to the people, but then got so bogged down in trying to pass huge, bundled legislation that none of them agree upon, nothing got done.

"OK, now those of you running to your churches right now, we really must talk! You are hearing directly from the God Center. Do you understand this?

"We watched in horror as over the millennia people have been slaughtered, tortured, displaced, disowned all in the name of God. In our name you killed, and you felt justified in doing so. Religious leaders imposed 'God's will', assuming they knew what God's will is. Honestly, we could hardly believe what you were doing, but why you did what you did was appalling. Do not fear us because we did not come to punish you, but rather to save you!"

In Russia, all guard units were rushing to protect their leader at the Kremlin. People in the streets were looking up at the pods and listening intently as the God Center dissolved their government.

"Dictatorship is not leadership," the God Center declared in Russian. People were cheering in the streets, tears flowed from many. "People, you will have representation in each district, and we are leveling the playing field in terms of finances and all of you will have the opportunity to live well in your newly adjusted country."

As the God Center went on in addressing the government officials, their leader was screaming orders to the guards and not paying attention. He was removed after a warning. The guards, being so shocked to see him just disappear, decided instantly to listen to the voice especially since in addition to their leader disappearing, so did their weapons. The God Center knew how to command attention.

Back in the U.S. the God Center continued.

"So many belief systems! We made you creative beings but when it comes to God, everyone is nuts. We have come to tell you all, once and for all time, you have missed the boat, so to speak. You have divided yourselves into 4200 different religions. What? Do you not see the insanity? And you fight over this? You are all spiritual energy beings having a human experience on a planet we put you on to manage. Amazingly you managed to mess this up. We are forgiving and we espouse only love, therefore, you get another chance. A bit of what you call 'tough love' is needed to get things running smoothly here.

"For the time being, until we straighten out everything down here on Earth, all church buildings will house the homeless for a few days. Yes, we see the homeless. Who do you think contacted us the most? The homeless! The God Center could not let this dysfunction on Earth continue.

"All of your man-made religions! Arguing and fighting amongst yourselves as to who is 'saved' and who is not. Seriously? We are here to save all of you from your own stupidity. The Vatican is receiving its orders from its own pod broadcast in Italian. This does not concern you right here, right now. But what will be revealed from their top-secret archives being made public will astonish you."

Jessie slid closer to Logan to whisper, "This will be something else! So much has been hidden from us I think the results are going to be shocking."

"Like this whole God Center isn't shocking?" Logan teased back.

The message continued.

"Everyone, that means truly everyone, has the same source. We hate to brag, but that source is us, the God Center. We are Love Energy. You all came from us. Now we see some of you are very distressed hearing this. You believed with all your hearts that your religion was 'the right' one.

"We are here to tell you that there is no organized religion on the face of this planet that is the 'right one'. We hear some fanatical Christians saying right now we are the devil, we are evil, we are spouting lies. We do understand you are struggling to comprehend what you believe are impossibilities.

"Please understand we are doing you all a favor. We came to save all of you. We are the only way this planet will go on. We are giving humanity another chance, an opportunity to live the way the God Center intended for you to live. This is the last chance for you. We are saving this planet and humanity on the planet for a makeover, a re-model, an intervention before you totally destroy yourselves and the planet. We are literally saving you from yourselves. We ask you to get rid of the stuff, the stories and old beliefs that keep you away from your one and only Source, us!"

"Wow this is going to crush the hell out of a lot of people!" Logan whispered to Jessie. Manuel had tears running down his face and Jessie, seeing this, put her arm around him. "Manuel, it will be okay. This is overdue if you ask me but hang in there."

"You all have free will so the choice is yours. Stay and witness the grand transformation we have for you or put your hand up to be removed. Removal will be instantaneous, painless and permanent. Just know that if you opt out now, you will truly miss the intended love and peace that will surround the Earth when our mission here is complete.

"If you cried for peace on Earth, you should stay. There will be peace on Earth. We know some just said the peace on Earth words because it seemed the thing to say. You bought Christmas cards with that being the theme. We know your hearts. There have been sincere pleadings for peace from some, others mouthed the words, but that desire was never prominent in their hearts. Too many of you profited greatly from wars so obviously you are not among the sincere hearts. The monies made, profits from wars, are being allocated elsewhere."

At the Pentagon, Manuel said "Interesting they are starting with the government. If we had been allowed to share what we know this wouldn't be such a surprise."

"I'm hoping they will reveal all the hidden secrets in the Vatican. Especially all the Mayan records which we've been told 'disappeared' just like the Maya people," Jessie sighed. Manuel and Logan nodded in agreement.

"If they do, indeed, have that information hidden it is beyond time for everyone to hear it. Of course, that will potentially destroy the majority of religions on Earth. Those studying ancient cultures won't be surprised since we've had visitors for over 5000 years, and it is how we came to be here. The many creative stories out there about creation are pretty much shot to hell," Logan added.

"Oh, my family won't take this well. They are all so Bible-based. I've tried for years to educate them with historical data, but I've been told to shut my heathen mouth!" he chuckled.

The Director approached Logan. "You were expecting this? You never indicated anything of this nature."

"Director, we didn't know this would happen. But we have presented many reports about the surveillance. If this is the God Center as the voice purports, and we are clearly outnumbered as well as having no control of whatever weaponry we have, paying attention to what the God Center says is key," Logan replied to the director then turned his gaze back to the screens, dismissing the director.

St. Vincent Cathedral was overflowing with people-frightened people weeping softly and others appalled at the message, struggling to understand. What the God Center was saying about their religion, about all religions was very extreme.

Father Gregory sat on the steps leading up to the altar where he'd served mass for over fifteen years. Incredulous as he pondered his decades of serving as a priest, and he was stunned at the thought his whole life was wrong. The shock of hearing what the God Center had said emptied his capacity to comfort others.

His hands were pressed together in the praying position as he looked up to the ceiling painted with cherubs, clouds and mythological characters that appeared to be in a battle. Odd that he never really saw that there were battles going on right on the church ceiling. That realization made him temporarily breathless, as tears began to run down his cheeks. He felt terribly alone.

But he was not alone. Hundreds were with him in the church, some even sitting there on the steps with him, yet he felt alone in his heart. Nobody spoke, but there were muffled sounds of crying and sniffling during the broadcast which continued on for some time. Homeless people began to enter with their bags and carts and the parishioners made room in the pews and aisles, not as much as a welcoming gesture as to avoid their odoriferous presence.

The communication continued from the God Center.

"The other major destructive area on Earth has to do with medicine and food. We made available during our creation of this planet, every possible plant and food for you to not just survive but thrive. There were some masters of this, the Chinese and Native Americans for two good examples. Knowing this is America we are addressing, no sense in making you uncomfortable talking about the Chinese right now since falsely you think they are your enemy. You have no enemies but yourselves!

"So let's talk about the Native Americans. You know, the Indians slaughtered or displaced due to your misunderstanding their culture. They possess the most complete natural apothecarial knowledge in this country. Their knowledge of herbs, plants, flowers and trees is fabulous. Early in United States history, some of the early pioneers did learn bits and pieces of their medicinal expertise. It was working well until along comes greed and power. A few very wealthy men, who were greed/power motivated and certainly not God- inspired individuals, came up with a huge money-making scheme.

"They had laboratories mimic the properties of the plants, flowers, roots and bark used as natural remedies so they could patent them. Fortunes were made from selling their imitation medicines. Need examples? The foxglove plant was morphed into their drug digitalis. Aspirin was created from mimicking elements of the spirea plant and willow bark. We could go on and on, but rest assured, this original medicine will be readily available, as intended.

"Then these same greedy gents went about changing the curriculum at all the medical schools by going away from anything natural that had been used in the past to using only their laboratory-created pharmaceuticals. It became fast growing and highly profitable for those involved. Then they mounted a huge campaign to totally discredit anything that was not coming from their laboratories. The real natural medicines were denounced as quackery in their greedy quest to control money and power."

The God Center wants to teach the people how to thrive by eating real living foods. For many, all the changes coming about are going to be received as a harsh reprimand. The God Center knows there is a fine line between creating anew and destroying things. This is all being done out of love for humanity, but it is not exactly being received that way. Truly it is tough love.

Food sources in many countries are compromised and polluted. Soils have been stripped of their naturally occurring nutrients from the overuse of chemicals. Few organic farms existed anymore. Peoples everywhere ingested chemicals through their foods and wondered how the general health of everyone was deteriorating.

The broadcast went on.

"We were watching this development of pharmacology in the God Center. Whenever humanity tries to replace things, we have created in the natural world with their pitiful imitations, it backfires. Oh, those companies are ridiculously profitable and the CEO of each is a millionaire. Good for them. How about the poor folks who cannot afford their drugs? How about the people who cannot take these imitations without medical complications?

"We have a serious intervention and do-over for the entire medical community. This is all tied up with another industry – insurance. We are here to ensure that in a perfectly run world, one should not need insurance for their health. How money centered everyone has become!"

Shandra Owens grabbed a tissue from her nightstand as she lounged in her bed listening. She couldn't help but cry. She had been rationing her diabetes medicines and feeling the ill effects. The hope she was now feeling about her future health provided her the energy to get out of bed.

Shandra had been struggling with her diabetes for the last four years. At 24, she did not think she would make it to 30. She worked full time as a cashier at Target and was trying to get her nursing degree at the community college part time. She had just missed an entire semester because she was experiencing fatigue, either from the drugs or the diabetes, she wasn't sure.

"Mama, did you hear that?" she shouted as she went downstairs to the kitchen. "If medicine will be free, I can take my insulin every day, no worries!"

"Oh Shandra, I've been prayin' so long for some help! Come sit with me, and we'll listen together." Many people, fighting illnesses they were told required medication for life were elated. At last – hope!

"Children of God, and you all are of course, everyone has the right to abundance, but things have developed here on your planet that are simply too out of balance. You're paying people millions to play football, or baseball and yet the sweet nurse who cares for you when you're ill makes peanuts comparably? Is this just? Is this fair? The teachers who educate your children make less than one hundred grand yet your football coaches average over a million dollars. We have much work to do here on Earth to get you back to basics and level the playing field.

"The God Center pondered the dysfunction we saw, knowing we could just blow up the planet and start over with humanity on another planet. But we know there is a global community of spiritual people we are extremely in love with carrying our love and peace in their hearts. We simply could not destroy them. We need them to help the rest of you make the necessary adjustments and changes here, especially to get over your attachment to your religion clubs.

"We love all of you, which is why we're here. So, we are here to help you set things right, the way the God Center intended. To do that, a lot will be destroyed in the process. What comes out of the destruction is akin to a forest burning down so new growth can sprout."

Americans spent $535 billion on prescription drugs in 2018, an increase of 50 percent since 2010. These price increases far surpass inflation, with Big Pharma increasing prices on its most prescribed medication by anywhere from 40 percent to 71 percent from 2011 to 2015.

Despite having the most expensive health care system, the United States ranks last overall compared with six other industrialized countries –Australia, Canada, Germany, the Netherlands, New Zealand and the United Kingdom.

Prescription drugs are a nightmare for poor and elderly people who could not afford them. Government promised to "look into this" but nothing is being done about it. For those particular groups of people listening, this broadcast brought relief and smiles. At last, they thought, somebody is doing something to help me.

The broadcast continued.

"We see and hear a lot of you discussing this now, arguing, crying, debating, getting fearful of what life is going to be like. Please stay calm. We will be here a while. This is not something to be done overnight. It took you hundreds of years to get this disheveled. We may be the

God Center, but this is a complicated world with billions of people. Everything will be taken care of.

"Perhaps we should have come sooner but we were hoping that you would get your act together. Given that you haven't, we are here to restructure and re-prioritize for everyone. So please stay calm and continue to listen to all we have to say. When we are done addressing the issues, the work will begin.

"Since this is being broadcast live, there will be no media 'interpretation' of what we are saying. You are hearing this directly from the God Center. There are no double meanings, there is nothing to interpret. We do not want Fox saying one thing and MSNBC taking it another way. There is only one way. It is the God Center way. Truth. Period. Just listen.

"We see you still aiming rockets. Oh please, people! Can you not just listen? We cut the power to them. We see you attempting to send drones up to our pods. You won't see anything so just stop it. We are here to stay until all the changes have been explained thoroughly, implementing as we go along new rules and procedures.

"Some of you have put your hands up to be removed. Are you sure? We know who you are. Most of you will do so well in a new Earth that we hesitate to remove you right now. When we are done addressing issues that must be changed, if you still want to be removed, poof and you're gone. Hear us out first, then decide. We will know who is truly heartfelt in their desire for this renovation of life on this planet.

"There will be no drugs to become addicted to anymore. We have removed them as easily and unceremoniously as you will be should you choose not to stay here. The other addicts, the food ones, will also be in for surprises, as is the entire food manufacturing industry. Wow, this one is really out of order.

"People are sick from the pretend food being manufactured. We call it chemical food. You drink soda. Ugh. You know what is in it, don't you? Absolutely nothing your bodies need. Expect your car to run on orange juice? Just saying. Proper performance means proper fuel. This junk is most prevalent in the United States, but for people elsewhere, like the European area, it is not as widespread.

"If you are in a grocery store hearing this, you will be witnessing more than half of the contents of the store disappearing. What will be left is not only safe to eat, but also what you should be eating in the first place. Honestly, we cannot even believe you have to be told this. We did equip humans with brains. But there are some very clever marketing 'geniuses' out there who have fooled you into thinking wrong thoughts. Some people are rather cavalier about their food choices, and too lazy to read labels. Notice something please. The food the God Center gives you does not require labeling."

As the broadcast from the God Center continued, the views on the screens changed to show people inside of a grocery store.

At a Publix grocery store in Tampa, shelves were emptied in a flash. Most of the canned goods were still there but the aisles of cereal, the beverage aisle, snack foods and yogurt were nearly empty.

Ken Jarmon, the manager of the store, stood in the empty aisle of cereals with his mouth open.

"OMG, it's really disappeared! I cannot believe this! There are maybe four cereals to choose from now. What will people buy?"

His mind went immediately into profit mode, but a flash of guilt hit him. Think of the bigger picture, he told himself as the broadcast continued. Then in a flash, the empty shelves filled with fruits and vegetables as the broadcast continued.

"No worries", the God Center continued, "there will be no debate on this food issue. Look at the obesity rate. Look at the diabetes rates climbing. The whole GMO (Genetically Modified Organism) thing. What GMO really means is God Move Over. Guess what? God is not moving over. Playing God in your laboratories? GMOs have contaminated the Earth and are contaminating its people. The God Center provided food for all to live on and that's what you should eat."

The screens then showed the various CAFO's (concentrated animal feeding operations). There were cows dragging their infected and swollen udders on the ground, as they made their way to the milking machines, chickens packed so tightly in low-ceiled buildings they couldn't walk. The scenes were horrifying, and the people didn't want to witness this, turning their heads away in disgust as the broadcast continued.

"Do you think the God Center likes to see cattle, pigs, chickens and the like in your confined animal farms, these CAFO's you call them? Is that the way to treat God's creations? Confined, fed drugs, living in feces, and sick is certainly wrong on many fronts and it will no longer exist.

"To make this insanity worse, chickens are raised like this, shipped to China for processing and then brought back to your grocery shelves. No more! When we said re-do, makeover and changes, believe us. Your food will be safe, locally grown as much as possible and free from chemicals."

In grocery stores everywhere, empty shelves were filling up with fruits and vegetables increased to such an excess that some shelves were overflowing. The God Center did this intentionally so nobody would enter a half empty store and panic.

This was going on globally, but the biggest changes were again mainly in the United States. Areas needing the most improvements were low-income neighborhoods where cheap junk food was the mainstay of their existence. Most there were not well acquainted with fresh fruits and vegetables. They would be now.

"While the existing technology you created isn't all bad, communicating has suffered, relationships have suffered and believe it or not, your brains are suffering. This will be one of the last things that we get into. We are very interested in seeing how the other industries and you yourselves deal with the changes. If technology proves valuable going forward, we may just tweak a few things to make it safer and better for you. If it is something that is in the common good to be improved upon, we will do so. If it seems to harm or not be in the common good for all, it may be eliminated. Use it wisely while we go through the redo of everything else. We see and hear all things. You cannot hide, even you, this country's president in your safe little bunker.

"You, President, unknowingly perhaps, have called attention to the Justice system. What a makeover is in store. It takes a ridiculous amount of time and money in your present system. Why? Too much bureaucracy, red tape, and sadly money rules again. If someone can afford a good lawyer, they get one. Otherwise, jail? And the wealthy get away with things, using influence, politics and money. It's a disaster. Oh yes, we will get into this, and it is not looking good for you personally, Mr. President!

"This planet has it all, or it did at one time, and we are here to restore it and humanity. If you feel the need to pray to God right now, just talk to your heart. We are there. Our pods will stay in place and the global broadcasts will become more sporadic as we address various countries, some individually.

"We will send you human helpers as needed to be right there with you to make changes. They are our representatives, and you must listen to them, respect them and learn. For example, we will send help for retrofitting manufacturing companies to make other or better products, fixing the housing crisis, creating a functional simplified version of your government and so on. We want this to be a peaceful transition."

The chambers of government were abuzz with discussions. Nobody was quiet, everyone talking at once, and anger was present. Snipets of conversations varied in responses.

"I just got $400,000 for my campaign. What do I do with it? Give it back? I need that money to run again!" one senator said.

"I am going to retire. I have enough in my investments to live comfortably," said another.

"You won't get that salary though. Probably not the retirement benefits either! Everything is being taken away from us!" whined another.

After some time of this verbal chaos, the leader of the Senate banged on the gavel and called the Senate to order.

"It seems we have been presented with an ultimatum. We either work for $300 per week, which is nonsense, or we walk out. Can anyone here survive with that income?" he asked indignantly. He removed his glasses because of the sweat racing down his face. Ordinarily he was well groomed and in cool control of himself. Wiping his brow again with the handkerchief from his jacket pocket, he noticed his hands trembling and hoped that nobody saw this. It would potentially ruin his reputation as a cool head under pressure. His own level of confidence was slipping. He had a lot to lose. Millions.

"I have investments to live on and I could sell one of my houses." shouted one senator.

"I'm staying. I'm sure y'all could do the same thing." Senator Highland was almost as wide as he was tall. But in this rotund body was a generous heart. People tended to come to him with problems and advice which he welcomed with his Zen approach rooted in gratitude. He often spoke about helping the less fortunate, probably because he came from an austere background. Becoming a senator had benefited him greatly and he had a bit of guilt hiding behind his good intentions.

Grumbling and rumbling ensued.

The gavel banged again.

"We have no idea what life is going to be like after this makeover. I'm too old to go through a total life makeover. I want to take a roll call of everyone. If you are choosing to stay, say 'Staying' or if you are quitting, retiring or whatever, say 'Leaving'. Now you don't have to make this decision immediately. Go home to your family and talk it over. Look at your finances. We are supposed to be working for the people not dancing for corporate funding, which is now ending. We will reconvene at nine tomorrow morning and vote on this. I need to know who is up for this challenge, and this certainly will be a challenge. Senate adjourned." He wanted desperately to go home, meet with his wife and see what they had squirreled away. Both had prestigious positions, and huge money connections, his mostly from pharmaceutical companies, hers from shady real estate transactions.

Congress, too, was bustling with debates, arguments and talk of resignations. Cell phones were working now that the broadcast was temporarily over and many were crying on the phone, or arguing, or debating about the choice they'd been given. There was no order for hours until one member went to the podium, banged a gavel and spoke, shouting above the din.

"Look people, this is chaos for sure. We've just been handed something clearly out of the blue and it is hard to wrap our heads around what is happening here. I, for one, am in this to stay. I'm nobody's hero, but I was elected to serve and serve I will. It's going to be tough financially, but I think this should be the least of our worries since everything on Earth is about to change so drastically. And maybe this is a good thing. I'm in. Let's vote and see if anyone else will stay with me. Please take your seats." said Mary Reynolds. She was a spokesperson known for her cool demeanor and reasonable approach to problems.

A vote was taken. Out of 532 elected officials, roughly two-thirds were present. And of those, 213 voted to stay, the rest abstained to vote later after discussions with their families. It was determined that they, too, would vote again in the morning.

The House of Representatives, as chaotically upset as they were, decided to table the vote until morning.

This prompted the silver orb over Washington to pipe up with a broadcast just for the Capitol.

"I see all branches of government need some time to confer with others to decide anything. This says to me that there are some doubts about how you will manage your lives without all those perks and 'extra' money coming in. Well, good! Think about it. But tomorrow is it.

"I know how you all like to take forever to pass legislation but that's because you had other factors to consider, like how much money you can make or not make as a result of your decisions. You know very well that is not why you were elected. You are to serve the people, to represent what is best for all, not best for you and your lake house, your vacations, your reserved dining, parking and so on.

"Tomorrow is it. Decide what is best for all, not just you and that mistress you are hiding, Trevor. Oh my! Yes, we see all, know all and frankly we know already what the vote is, but we will give you time until tomorrow. You will find a printout of your benefits on your desks in the morning. When you are ready, we will send a representative to help you establish a new government. The people will love it Try to remember that is who you all work for!!"

Logan missed his dentist appointment but laughed it off. He doubted that with the God Center appearance a hell of a lot of things didn't

24

happen today as scheduled. He'd been at the Pentagon for 17 years, brought in because of his outstanding credentials as an astrophysicist with NASA.

When the broadcast was over, a few people still sat staring at the screen while the majority made a beeline for their offices.

"This really explains a lot, doesn't it? Especially like hiding things in order to perpetuate lies. Area 51 needs to come clean, and the Vatican, hell the whole government!" Logan said as they were trying to figure out what to do next in the 'intelligence' department.

Jessie, Logan's assistant, had a background in anthropological sciences and had traveled to countries with ancient ruins and standing stones. The stones dated back more than 5000 years, some could be 12,000 or more. They were plentiful on the planet, numbering over 50,000, mostly in Europe, Asia, South America and various islands.

One of her favorite spots was Rudston England, perhaps because she was born in London forty-one years ago.

The standing stone there is 50 feet tall. The amazing part of this standing stone, twenty-five feet of it is above ground, while the other twenty-five feet is below ground. How did that ever come to be? It is made up of gritstone which has conductivity due to the quartz in the composition. It is possible that this was a part of a wireless energy grid some have speculated.

Ancient physics, which was and is, more advanced than what is known today, has a lot to do with the standing stones. Especially in Carnac, France, the sight of one of the extensive Neolithic menhirs (a tall upright stone erected in prehistoric times) collections in the world. There are several "stories" as to why and how they are lined up the way they are, more than 10,000 of them, in 11 rows for a mile. Interestingly, when viewed from above they make a Pythagorean Theorem, which is a triangle that is useful for two-dimensional navigation. Fascinating that

Pythagoras didn't come up with the theorem until the seventh century and the stones were there centuries before he existed.

"I'm really excited about this. We could be getting answers to things we have wondered about for centuries! And you know I've heard it said that when it comes to physics, we only know about 20% of what some of the ancients knew. That's why we can't figure out how the pyramids were built or any of the multi-ton standing stones." Jessie said as the trio walked the corridors to their office.

"I need a drink!" said Manuel. "Do you guys want to join me?"

"Ordinarily I would, Man, but I need to go home and tend to the family's reaction to all this." Logan replied.

Logan was 57, married for 27 years to the love of his life, Patti and they had two sons. Logan knew his Catholic wife needed him to come home and he texted her when he left the conference room. The phones were off during the broadcast, but Logan knew she would be working herself up. He smiled to himself knowing there would be a lot of discussions in homes all over the world tonight. Indeed, this was life changing and for everyone, not just a few.

Jessie begged off as well.

"Well, if the liquor store hasn't been raided, I guess I'll bring a bottle home to help me through the hysteria I know awaits me!" Manuel lamented.

It was a rush hour nightmare getting from the Pentagon to his home. He took the blue line of the metro to the suburb of Clarendon. He walked the three blocks from the station to his brick Georgian home, looking up at the stars with a renewed reverence. Changes were coming, big changes. He was not feeling the least bit fearful but rather a long-sought peace that things would indeed change but for the betterment of mankind and the planet.

Patti rushed at him as soon as he entered the front door, hugging him and crying. He held her tenderly, smoothing her long brown hair with his steady hands.

"It's all going to be okay, Patti. I know this is upsetting but honey, we are going to find out the truth of so much. No more mysteries! No more lies!" he said in his most comforting tones.

Patti had been crying that was obvious. Her eyes were red and swollen. "Oh Logan, I cannot believe this is happening! What kind of lies are you talking about?"

"Let me tell you about Galileo. Come, let's sit down." as he ushered her into the living room to sit on the couch. Just then, their son Matt came in the front door.

"Are you okay, mom? I came over as quickly as I could. Traffic is a mess!" he said, coming into the room and hugging his mother.

"Mom will be fine, we all will be fine, Matt." Logan said, giving Patti a kiss on her tear-stained cheek. "Come sit with us, Matt. I was just about to explain some things."

"Did you know about this? Did you know this was going to happen?" Matt inquired somewhat angrily.

"No Matt, I didn't know for sure this would happen, but we have been under surveillance for a very long time and sooner or later contact had to happen. We are so fortunate it is not a warlike invasion but rather one of peace and love. If the God Center had not announced this message and taken control of our weaponry, we would have attacked first and asked questions later. My God, it would have been like the Fourth of July!

"Anyway, I was about to tell Mom about Galileo. He was an astronomer and scientist. Back in 1633 his world of science collided with the world of scholasticism and absolutism that held power in the Catholic Church. He believed the Earth revolves around the sun. For that he was brought to trial and sentenced to life imprisonment. You see the Catholic Church declared, quite unscientifically, that the Earth was the very center of the universe, and all revolved around Earth."

"Dad, what the hell does that have to do with the invasion?" Matt demanded.

Logan smiled at the question but knew he had to stay calm and explain. "While I have respected your mother's right to be a Catholic, that religion elevated itself beyond and above all else as the number one source of all knowledge in the world. And this knowledge they declared was from God and therefore infallible. The Vatican didn't admit its error until 1992, when most people were not paying attention, or didn't know the Galileo story in the first place. Most people could have cared less what happened so long ago and yet it is a perfect example of the arrogance of the church and the lengths it goes to stay in control of people, pretending to know everything about everything.

"For them to admit error in anything at all is monumental. But more information will come out now, some has already, to debunk the religious stories that have controlled people for centuries." Logan replied. Secretly he was glad this would be the end of any future agitation about going to church with his wife. Logan felt there was a supreme source, but organized religions turned him off.

Patti pushed Logan away, releasing herself from his embrace. "Haven't you just been waiting for this day? Now you can blast away at religion!"

"Patti, honey, listen, I didn't orchestrate this nor am I telling the God Center what to say. I am so sorry that this is hitting you so hard and I will try to do whatever I can to help you." Logan said, reaching for her hand. She didn't pull away further but squeezed his hand.

"I know Logan. But all my life…."

"Patti, you've always believed in God. Well, we are getting it right from God now, all the information, all the revealing of what we should have known. I have more hope for this planet and all of humanity now more than ever, ever before. Can we go fix some food? I'm really hungry. I obviously missed my dentist appointment today, which screwed me out of lunch."

"This is like the movie "The Day the Earth Stood Still," Matt said.

"No, it's not at all. We are getting communication from them, and in the movie, there was no voice saying what's happening. I think that's what made the people in the movie panic so much because they were afraid. The God Center is communicating and telling us exactly why they are here and what they are going to do. It's not an invasion, from a warlike source. It's a life-saving mission, saving our lives and the planet. Look, if this planet dies, so do we!"

"Yeah, I guess your right dad. Let's go find something to eat, I'm starving too," Matt said.

The three wandered into the kitchen while Patti took sandwich fixings out of the fridge. She had planned on a casserole, but the broadcast changed everyone's plan for the day and for their lives.

Logan and Patti had been through a lot together. His father died in Tower One on 9/11. His mother had a stroke two years later and Patti and Logan brought her to live with them and they took care of her. His mother died the following year. Their eldest son, Michael went into the Air Force after attending the Academy in Colorado and Patti missed him terribly. He would come home every now and then from his travels, but it was never a long visit or enough for his mother. She was glad Matt was living in the area.

Later that evening, Logan and Patti cuddled in bed. "I know I've been a mess over this, Logan. I'm sorry. What do you think will happen to your job? I've been so self-absorbed and haven't been thinking of how this will affect you," Patti said.

"Honey, I just don't know. Everyone's wondering the same thing. I figure I will trust the God Center to work things out since who knows more than God, huh?" Logan said as he gave her a tight hug.

"You're so calm about all this Logan. I mean I am glad one of us is, but your career?" she couldn't finish her sentence. Tears were welling up again and she did not want to cry again.

"We'll be fine, sweetheart. You know we had a mess on Earth, especially our country, so I am going to remain optimistic that all the fuck ups will be remedied. Let's be happy, Patti. Our sons will not be going to war. We're safe, we're together, and we're in good health. Give me a kiss goodnight and let's get some sleep. We don't know what will happen tomorrow, so let's get some sleep so we are ready for it," Logan said as he kissed his wife and rolled over to go to sleep.

As usual, Logan went to sleep quickly, and Patti tossed and turned her mind a jumble of thoughts. Lies? On purpose? How did this ever happen? Patti had an entire night of questions, as did millions of others. Was this really heaven sent?

When you cannot control what's happening, challenge yourself to control the way you respond to what's happening. That is where your power is.

Buddha

DAY TWO

The night was not altogether peaceful. In Georgia a few inebriated men used all their ammunition shooting at the orb that was nearby. They were simultaneously removed.

In New York, traders spent the night at the stock exchange, sleeping on the floor waiting for whenever the exchange would be reactivated. Debates, arguments, fist fights took place there and in several bars across the country.

At the Cieslak home, Logan slept peacefully despite the thrashing around that indicated Patti was not in a peaceful state.

Before Matt had left his mom last night, he reminded her that he was raised to always tell the truth in every circumstance. "Mom, sometimes they say the truth hurts and I can see you are hurting. I'm a little confused about all this myself, but we should honor the truth and be grateful we are at last getting some truth. Please mom, no more crying. We want the truth and its coming, even the truth you didn't know about, like your church."

"Oh Matt, I'll calm down, I promise. Be safe going home and thanks for coming over." Patti had talked to her other son, Michael, who lives in Japan on assignment with the Air Force earlier. He, too, knew that his very strictly Catholic mother would be falling apart with the revelations of truth coming out. Michael considered himself Catholic because that was how he was raised, but he wasn't actively involved with

Catholicism since he left home. He made his mother feel a bit better by letting her know it was peaceful in Japan with the orbs. People were listening and there was no panic.

Logan woke up to find that Patti was already up and he could smell the coffee brewing in the kitchen. Patti was always up with the sun, no matter what time they went to bed. He appreciated her stealth exit from the bedroom every morning, and really loved getting up to fresh brewed coffee. When he got into the kitchen, Patti smiled, grabbed a mug and poured his coffee.

"Do I smell a fire in the fireplace?" he asked.

"Yes, as a matter of fact. I couldn't sleep last night so I went to the library in the den. Found a dozen books I felt needed burning," she offered rather coyly.

"Oh? What books, dare I ask?" Logan inquired.

"I think you know Logan. I am no longer a Catholic, I am a child of God, and God is the one and only creator of life, of my life. All the rituals, rules, and stories I was taught are burning as we speak," she said. "I couldn't sleep last night. I was very busy coming up with a plan for myself. Obviously, I cannot control what is going on. All I can control is my reaction. Rather than boo-hoo, I'm accepting this. Here is God himself telling us that none of the religions are right. My gosh, you cannot fight this, so I'm doing what I must to get over it. I saved the family tree pages from the front of the Bible, but the rest is burning."

Logan smiled. She would be okay. He wondered if the people in the Bible belt would do as well as Patti in acceptance.

"Can you call the dentist for me and reschedule my appointment for next month? I think the next few weeks may be more than a little busy and chaotic for me. I'm going to the office today, but I have no idea yet how long that will be my office. I don't know for sure what any of us will be doing in the future until the God Center arranges everything. I'm trying to be flexible; I think we all should be, don't you?" he asked Patti.

"Yes of course. So, you really don't know if your task force will be needed, or where you'll work, or even if your team will stay together?"

"No, not yet. But I'm really excited, like this is going to be a new world we live in and the end of bull shit hopefully," Logan said looking into his coffee mug as a tea leaf reading psychic would.

Patti noticed that and laughed. "Logan, the answers aren't going to be in your coffee!" she said hugging him.

Relieved at her affectionate gesture, Logan put the mug down and gave her a tight hug. "It's all going to be fine, Patti. I just know it. Changes sure, but I'm feeling it's all positive. We will adjust just fine."

Changes had been made literally overnight that astounded people everywhere on the planet. One of the biggest in Washington DC was at the Pentagon. One wing of it had already been converted into apartments on all five floors. People who had worked in that wing had been directed to clean out their personal belongings before they left on day one. They were told to go home but to be on call for future assignment. The God Center has everything worked out so people will still have jobs, they might be doing something else entirely, but they will work.

Out of the more than 25,000 people, mostly military, working at the Pentagon, few questioned the God Center's representatives who were dressed in white from head to toe. There was a glow about them that made some people very uncomfortable.

One robust colonel shouted a lot of profanities, said this was a declaration of war and he would not give in to it since his whole career was fighting what he was told was evil.

"We are not evil, and this is not war," said one representative. "Your cooperation is appreciated because we have much work to do to convert the Pentagon into living quarters for the elected government officials. You may go home and await further orders, colonel."

"I answer only to the President of the United States I'll have you know," he said angrily.

"And we, sir, answer to God. We believe the Ultimate Commander in Chief, God, who is in charge, not your president," replied the representative. "Please pack your belongings now and go home to await further orders."

"I have top secret clearance and there are things in this office you may not touch," screamed the colonel.

Hearing that, a few other in offices nearby came to help usher the indignant colonel out of his office and his screams could be heard down the long corridors. No matter what happened, there were always those who fought and resisted. The silver pods had been cursed at, shot at and screamed at globally, in many languages by people who could not accept the reality of what was happening.

In Russia, the guards who immediately had surrounded the Kremlin dispersed as soon as their weapons vanished. How can one protect anything without weapons?

Likewise in China, without their weapons, the Chinese Liberation Army, all 2.5 million of them, had no weapons suddenly. Their top leaders, as in Russia, were removed and the new government was being created by the God Center representatives. The soldiers everywhere went home, awaiting further instructions from their newly created leadership.

At this period of time on Earth, mankind was hostile and rebellious before the God Center had arrived and for some that negative outlook was exacerbated by the presence of the God Center.

Screams of "Dictator!" were not uncommon. Pity those that would not listen to God with an open mind and heart. The God Center knew many would be removed from the planet in order to ensure peace would stand a good chance. It also wanted to give everyone a chance, for some a second chance, to show where their heart was.

At the capitol building with the majority of elected officials present, the voting roll call began. The grids of silver discs or pods were still in place, ever watchful even when quiet.

In the Senate, missing only two senators, fifteen decided to take early retirement, fully aware that the perks they thought they had coming were now nearly non-existent. They would receive a one-time retirement payment of $100,000 and that was it. Their social security income would be based on whatever income they had before becoming a servant of the people. For the 'career politicians' it wouldn't amount to much at all.

Seventy-five senators decided to serve the one year before the mandatory elections would be held. A majority of them would not run for re-election but were already trying to line up jobs outside of government, some ironically with their corporate donors.

By the end of the day, four senators would put their hands up. They had made the decision to be removed since they thought that the cushy life they had was over and they were unable to tolerate the changes to come.

In Congress, there were similar percentages, but not without impassioned speeches.

"I came into government to make government better. I see what folly my personal ambition was for this job. So, what happens? God intervenes. I mean a here-and-now intervention, as in person as it gets and I'm still trying to comprehend the explosive nature of the last twenty-four hours. It's like some science fiction movie. I couldn't sleep last night wondering how many of my colleagues are staying to fight the good fight for the people of this great nation. I truly do believe we can make this nation better than ever and I am willing to make the sacrifice to see that happen. I hope, truly hope, that you will all be with me in this challenge," said a congressman from Massachusetts.

"I never believed in God. I don't know what the fuck is going on with this space brigade coming here like this, but I'll be damned if I am going to see everything I worked my ass off for just go poof in the night. I am not staying for whatever bullshit make-over this silver orb in the sky has in mind," shouted the angry congressman from Texas. Sadly, several cheered him on to raise his hand. He was always angry about something and not well liked by his peers. He would not be missed.

It was a day of speeches. A few women cried as they spoke, seemingly more upset about their religion being tanked, than their job issue. So many people prided themselves on being Christians or Catholics and they identified with their religious affiliations. They shared their feelings of being "totally lost" without their religion as part of who they were, so much so during this session, that the God Center had to speak up.

"You are our children, you know. We understand you are having a hard time with this religion thing. You have not lost anything. We are the God Center. We want only for you to thrive on Earth. We made all of you. You have not lost God. We are right here talking to you! It's all the trappings, all the stories you created in the name of God that you became addicted to. All the while you continued separating yourselves with your labels. All the labels! The God Center is unifying the human species into one peaceful, loving, tolerant-of-all planet. Don't you want to experience the Oneness?

"Oh my dear ones please listen to us. You may be confused because we are using the plurals of we and us instead of saying 'I this' and 'I that'. For you, your concept of God may be singular in nature. Understandable. Completely. The God Center is made up of Joy, Light, Creativity, Intelligence, Laughter, Honesty, Loyalty, Peace, Harmony, Trust, Integrity, and the big one LOVE. We are that, I AM THAT, all that, so it really is plural, you see?

As the God Center continued, the voice changed. Now it was a female voice. "We are all inclusive. The God Center is not just male or female, we are everything. Perhaps that will end the question 'Is God a woman or a man:' because your answer is yes. We are everything.

"We sent you many Earthly messengers, you know. Buddha, Mohamed, Jesus to name a few. They all carried messages directly from us. Somehow over time, people worshiped the messengers and created many stories around them. While we normally salute creativity, what did this do on Earth? Everyone has their own opinions, their own beliefs and certainly this has divided people up by what kind of religion they have, what church they go to and so on.

"*It's divisive*, don't you see that? Do you honestly think God wants you all divided up into religion clubs? Please. Because you all couldn't get this, we were forced to come down here and straighten you all out. Didn't you read Neal Donald Walsh? We spoke to him. He wrote it all down in a series called 'Conversations with God'. Cute title, don't you think? But seriously, did you read it?

"We have found that subtlety does not work, at least in the United States. We are here now, because this is the only way to save the Earth and humanity. It breaks our hearts that we had to go to this extreme to communicate with you all. We understand what a jolt we are giving you, but we are here now. You will learn, for once and for all, what really matters. You will witness more miracles in the coming days than any Bible book could contain. Yes, we know, we know, you've been told that it is the word of God. Those writings are the most misconstrued representations ever conceived by man. And not one man, but many men. If you understood what life was like when it was written, and the political winds, you could easily understand those were not our words.

"You want to be near to God? Are you deaf? Well, you cannot be. We made sure that the deaf on this planet were given hearing so they would understand everything that is happening. We are here, right here, right now."

That broadcast had a calming effect on the elected officials. At least for the moment, they decided to just go for the vote and stop with the speeches. After collecting the votes in Congress that were sent in from members not in Washington via text, the results were 468 staying for the year, 64 taking early retirement. No hands went up for removal.

The House of Representatives, after hearing the latest broadcast, went to vote quickly. 399 would stay for the year, with 36 'retiring'.

"And Government officials, all of you, this division with Republicans, Democrats and Independents fighting with each other over issues nobody is really dealing with, well, enough! You all work for the people you represent. If we see in the next few days, that you are still so partisan that things are not getting done, then government is not working for the people, we will dissolve the parties into one. We're watching you. And we will be supervising the setup of new procedures to actually do work for the people you serve."

Normally the media would have had a field day with this information, but the God Center made sure that there was silence from them for a few days. There were people in newsrooms across the country having nervous breakdowns, some very quietly, some raging on and on. They had no idea what their place would be in the make-over, or even if they had a place at all. With a grid of pods encircling the Earth with only one mile between them, broadcasts could be directed to wherever the God Center wanted. Seeing the distress, the God Center beamed out to the media specifically.

"Please calm down. I know this is all very unsettling and you are feeling extremely insecure about your futures. There will be a place for some media when we are done here. But there will be a true challenge for you. Call it New Rules.

"It really isn't new rules if you are a journalism major, which surprisingly few of you are. First, truth and facts, not opinions. People need to think for themselves without your personal opinion of everything. Come on, you know that some of the stuff you say is just to sell copy, get more viewers, sensationalizing things all the time, creating controversy and debate. Let me tell you something. A reporter is to inform people, not to give opinions, not to play politics. Few can say you are innocent. We have seen the polarization in this country grow because of your divisiveness, your blaming and accusations between channels, spewing lies, hatred and division. Hardly news reporting, is it?

"You have decisions to make about your careers. If you can toe the line, keep it clean, honest news, with absolutely no politics swaying your presentations then wait it out until we give you access to do so. If you are debating this issue with yourselves right now, as some of you are because we know everything, then leave this career and find something else, some other way to contribute to society.

"Everyone is going to contribute something, some talent or knowledge that they have to better things and help people. So, get a grip on the new reality and decide for yourself what you want to do. Let me warn you, if anyone, not just the media either, agrees to continue in the changes but then later starts any rebellion or meanness, you will be removed. We are not doing this again. We love you dearly. We are taking the time to personally clean up your planet on all levels. Nobody can ever say you 'didn't know' the requirements of cooperation. The whole world knows.

"We have observed only a few cases of looting. Stop this or you will find yourselves instantly removed. We are leveling the playing field so needs will be met for everyone. We see everything, as we continue to tell you, so think of the consequences of your intolerable behavior."

There was a renewed hush, with some "Wow, that was something!" spattered about in media centers around the country. Some were transcribing every word, or taping it on recorders, while others just looked to the ceiling or out the window to the nearest silver pod and listened. The collective shock of what was going on made a few wonder if they were having a nightmare.

Many knew they would be out of work, or at least maybe out of their present position. No political analysis news programs would be necessary. The management in their haughty offices sensed the changes coming would slash programming. Their main concern---money of course--- was the whole world of commercials. Who would pay for airtime to support their programming? The pharmaceutical industry was a huge advertiser on television. With Big Pharma being nearly eliminated altogether, then what?

"We know your concerns," said the God Center to television management in the sweet female voice. "In lieu of drug advertising, you will be allocated funding for broadcasting. There will still be companies that would like to advertise on your channels, but the price of doing so will be adjusted to reflect the new economy.

"Between reduced revenues and funding from the common good funds some of you will still have jobs. Salaries won't be the same across the board but most of the news conglomerates expanded and diversified into many other companies. We aren't eliminating news, just tailoring it to the people's needs; keeping in mind those needs are very basic, as long as you deal with truth. With all the channels, each taking their own stand on everything, did you honestly think you were contributing to anything but divisiveness? Simplicity is needed. Again, priorities have been very misaligned."

Hospitals were becoming over-run with drug addicts going through withdrawal. The God Center knew this would happen when the drugs disappeared. It wasn't just the drugs on the street that had disappeared. Drug cartels moving trucks of cocaine found their trucks empty, ships

with containers that had products hiding drugs in them, and every pill
bottle anywhere and everywhere that had harmful drugs in them were
now empty.

From the God Center directly to all hospitals came this message.

"We see many hospitals are fancy, with hotel-like lobbies, chandeliers,
fountains and some with entire walls of fountains. It's quite lovely. Who
paid for that? Was that Mrs. Wasserman's contribution? You billed her
insurance company $350,000 for her heart surgery and she has a second
mortgage on her home to pay you the balance of $90,000. Or is it all
the chemo patients coming for outrageous and expensive treatments
you know don't work?

"Big question for you. When did hospitals become for profit? How
can you be a human being profiting off of the sick and dying? Whose
brilliant idea was that? Oh, don't tell us, we know everything, we're just
trying to wake you up. Why have boards of directors? Corporations
use them to manage profits, expand business and increase income. You
don't need one.

"First of all, you will never, ever charge a patient ten dollars for
a Tylenol pill, a toothbrush, or a box of Kleenex like you have been.
Throw out your lists of what you are currently charging for everything.
That's history!

"Forget your profit. You aren't allowed profits in this field. How
can anyone hope to make money off the illnesses people have? We are
going to work it out with the corporations who previously have spent
millions on endorsing politicians to endorse hospitals instead. Some of
them, not all of them, will help you out, and some will be helping the
educational system.

"So, give us your actual operating expenses and you will be given
the funds. People will not pay you for anything and we don't want to
hear about insurance companies. For now, pretend they don't even exist
because they won't in the future, not for health. The God Center is

working on this angle. Our representatives will be at every hospital on the planet to direct you with all the obvious changes.

"All nurses need to be paid more. You know they are the breath of the hospital and without them you are not a hospital at all. Start out doubling their pay immediately, double again next year. Stop crying about the money. You'll have enough. Corporations are going to make a huge difference and so is the MLB, you know, the Major League Baseball. Everything will be getting streamlined financially. We want our children to get priorities right. MLB is entertainment. Nurses work long hard shifts and save lives. This should be easy to see. This is what we mean about priorities. It's common sense.

"Another thing, what is that on the dinner tray you're serving? Mystery meat? And why on Earth do you serve Jell-O? It's sugar. Do you know that sugar is bacteria's favorite? You are treating sick people with infections and people straight out of surgery with sugar foods? Oh my people please read some basic nutrition books and pitch the sugar! Hire some decent chefs to cook meals that people can eat, healthy food, good food that helps them heal. Food heals, you know. I guess you don't believe that, but you better start believing it. Half of the illness on this planet is due to chemical foods being manufactured, and then the chemicals sprayed on the crops. This combo causes diseases. Sugar is in everything here on Earth and needs to be revisited. It is killing you slowly.

"We think it's hysterical that the registered dietitian nutritionist or nutrition dietetic technicians whatever you are calling them these days, are controlled by the companies that fund them. Here's a few of the companies that support this association: McDonald's, PepsiCo, The Coca-Cola Company, Sara Lee, General Mills, Kellogg's, Mars, and, what do you know, The Sugar Association.

"Your hospitals hire these dietitians to plan the meals in a hospital? The Academy of Nutrition and Dietetics is the world's largest organization of food and nutrition professionals, and power is the name of the game they play. They have a history of vigilant persecution for anyone in the more 'natural' fields of nutrition, and much like the American Medical Association, it's a group of ego-centered righteous, intolerants who want to control everything. Follow the money once again. While the original intent of these associations may have come across as something good for the people, it's like a fox guarding a hen house to use one of your expressions.

"We have a lot of schooling and retraining for these folks, and the entire medical field. With only good healthy foods to choose from, you will all learn to eat healthy which eliminates their purpose. There shouldn't have to be an association of dietitians to tell you what to eat. Changes. Yes, many are needed here.

"The current medical profession has a one-way approach, considering anything else pure quackery. You treat with external rather than internal elixirs. The mind and body do the healing, not doctors, but sometimes their treatments help speed the process, but not necessarily in a positive direction."

Dr. Kendall Reid, a naturopathic physician and professor at Trinity College was listening to the broadcast in his classroom. He was happy to hear what the God Center was saying. His profession was constantly under attack as quackery and unorthodox. The school had to prepare their eager students for what might happen in their practices when they completed their schooling. He wanted to take this opportunity to reinforce this since the God Center was hopefully going to give many the boot.

"Class, I've told you before that the ADA (American Dietetic Association) is funded by food multinationals, pharmaceutical companies and food industry lobbying groups. Obviously for funding them, the

ADA is then pressured into approving and recommending whatever their benefactors want them to, like please endorse our garbage." Dr. Reid said.

"There was no denying problems exist in the food industry. Manufacturers hired chemists to enhance flavors, create flavors to make their chemical food products irresistible, even habit forming. These chemists discovered Aspartame by accident. The scientists at the FDA rejected it. Then, well what do you know? The head of the FDA was fired and replaced by someone who would green-light the product. Now it's in thousands of items. The FDA has quite a long list of complaints from people and doctors about the nasty side effects, but the product is still alive on grocery shelves. Why isn't anyone listening? Follow the money." he concluded. "People could learn this on their own just by going to YouTube, but they don't. This history of the AMA is there, and it isn't pretty."

They went on to their study of the amino acids with a renewed sense of purpose. The world would be open to the natural ways, the real God-created way. Allopathic medicine would not be eliminated totally but the re-education was critical. Few drugs' physicians used will remain. The toxic side-effects are not worth keeping them. They do not "cure" anything. All they do is eliminate some of the symptoms.

At the White House, the president was trying desperately to have a news conference. Being in the bunker he could not be in the spotlight. His problem was that there was no media he could summon. It was driving him bat shit crazy. He thrived on being in front of the cameras at least once or twice a day. Social media was out of play and there was no spotlight for him. In his utter frustration and against the sage advice of his staff, he went out on the balcony again to talk to the invaders.

"Aliens! I command you. Leave us right now. I have spoken to my military chiefs and the Pentagon, and we will fire on you ceaselessly until you leave or become ashes." the president yelled.

"Oh my people, no you did not. You have the audacity to lie to the God Center? You still don't get we are not invaders? In your head you might aspire to control the world and humility evades your person to a very dangerous level. You have spoken to the Pentagon, but after offering up some of the elements our silver pods are made of, your experts know full well you have absolutely nothing in your weapons arsenal that could ever harm our crafts. We know you live to be on the television. It doesn't matter what you say. Most of what you say is nonsense or lies anyway but you sure do love the camera."

"Why are you always saying, 'oh my people?' the president asked.

"It's the same for us as when you are saying oh my god, or OMG which we've heard millions of times today, I am God, so I can't say Oh my ME, can I? To you it's OMG and to me it's OMP, which means oh my people."

"I don't believe you're God! First a man's voice, and now a woman's voice. Prove you are God. Do something God-like." the president insisted.

"We've already done 'God-like' things all around you aren't you paying attention? You didn't believe in God before we came here. You fooled a lot of people into thinking you were a true believer. Some even think you are the Messiah, which really cracks us up by the way, and now you expect me to prove to you that we are the God Center? Wow. Go sit at your big desk in your big chair and make a list of all your big assets. You are acting like a child, having tantrums and making demands. Remember, we already know what your assets truly are, so this is a test for you, big guy. List them all and then we'll talk again."

"Well, you are not taking anything away from me. I don't even know who you are!" the president thundered back. He was among only a handful of leaders who at this point, still did not believe what was happening and thought they could control things.

There were 50 dictatorships or authoritarian regimes ruling millions and millions of people across the globe. All the dictators faced elimination if total cooperation was not given. Out of the 50, only 8 agreed to step down and be a part of the reconstruction. For the staffs, vice presidents and allies in the government offices to see their leaders just disappear as the God Center said they would, cooperation evolved quickly. Nearly all of the governments worldwide manipulate rather than serve the people. This is ending.

Addressing the remains of what was each government, the God Center had another point to make. "We want all governments in the future to know that each country will be set up cooperatively. Your land is your land, and you do not ever try to 'conquer' others. Each country has resources to share and trade. There will be no invading another country for any reason. We have been disappointed that Earth is one of the most warlike planets in the entire universe. This is not something you should be proud of. That is the main reason we have removed all of your destructive weaponry. There is no peace on Earth possible with your previous behaviors. Our representatives are working with all countries to set up a fair and honest, also vastly simplified government."

The God Center, directing their 'representatives" or angels, as some call them, spent time in particular areas of the globe with governments across the globe while simultaneously supervising the distribution of food in India and Africa. By controlling the weather on the planet, more was being restored. Lakes, rivers, farmlands had a resurgence of prosperity much needed by the people of the regions. Soon the people would prosper as well.

In Russia, the inefficiencies in the government apparatus stemmed from the high levels of corruption. The number of professionals wanting to leave the country is at 50% in certain areas. This condition affects the country's ability to attract foreign talent as well. This not only reduces the creative potential to support economic development but reduces domestic consumption. A major over-haul of their government was taking place. This was enough for the people of Russia to be positively jubilant. They were far more oppressed by their government than by their religions.

All screens, be they laptops, TV's, iPad or phones, showed the people scenes from around the globe so all could see the changes were beneficial. It helped so many of them accept the God Center was here to save the Earth, and fears were melting away.

Padma Varadkar saw the rain in the fields of her father's farm in rural India. She and her brother Patel ran outside to dance in the rain. Her mother, Najma watching her children so jubilant filled her heart with joy and love.

"Ah," she said to the silver pod hovering overhead, "you bring heaven to Earth! Thanks be to God!"

Najma knew without rain; their crops would fail again. She and her neighbors had already started communal food sharing, but even with that they were hungry. Her husband Aryan had just told her last week that he would leave the farm and go to the city for work if the crops failed again. She was overjoyed and grateful that they could stay, the farm would flourish again, and they would not go hungry.

There had been so many farmers in India committing suicide that people considered it an epidemic. When GMOs had been introduced there, claims of bigger yields producing more profits lured the farmers into the GMO cotton. After the cotton crops were harvested, the farmers let their livestock graze in the fields, as was the custom. It was an honest mistake that cost them all of their livestock. They died as a result of foraging in fields that had been heavily sprayed for the GMO cotton. As if life there wasn't hard enough, they'd lost everything. The prime minister upon hearing of this, wept. The company supplying the farmers with GMO seeds and weed-killing sprays denied any responsibility.

Globally, the God Center was getting more cooperation in restructuring. There were severe problems in South America with corrupt governments. Setting up the right people and procedures to run the countries was simpler once the antagonists were removed. Seeing this, as well as the terrorist gangs disappear, people celebrated in the streets. It was a jubilant time across much of the planet.

Perhaps the countries of the Middle East portion of the planet underwent the most immediate physical changes. In Iran, as soon as the God Center spoke of religions, leadership there was in shock and panic. The country had been run on Islamic rule tied to their religion, with constant tensions between the Shiite and Sunni communities. The government had repeatedly restricted or completely shut down mobile communication systems and the internet. It didn't matter as all could easily hear the broadcasts from the God Center. The sound of the voice was heard with or without Earthly communication devices. All the controls would end, giving people freedom. Sparing the women of the burka and giving them "rights" was long overdue.

The country has 9 million people illiterate out of 85 million. The God Center had hundreds of representatives going into Iran and the other countries needing restructuring and setting up educational centers. Education is considered 'holy' and the God Center wanted all people to be blessed with knowledge.

In Afghanistan, the Taliban shot at one of the representatives. It was the only shot fired there and did no damage. Their guns disappeared rendering their resistance inconsequential. The God Center informed all that elimination would be the consequence of any resistance going forward.

The people and the economy of the country had suffered due to the wars and the sanctions. Without transparency, corruption thrives. The lives of the government officials were quite luxurious compared to the squalor of most of the populations. Leveling the playing field there was a challenge only the God Center could handle. As things were quickly changing there, the wails of outrage came only from the wealthy.

The broadcast resumed.

"Everyone can see for themselves what is happening in many areas today as we are rearranging things and getting priorities where they need to be. Your screens will show you what is going on all over the planet. You can see for yourselves there are places where people are dancing in the streets because we have come to save you. There is no looting, nor violence. We want you to witness this global transformation. Especially those who are, for whatever reason, not able to accept this is the God Center. This is your one and only chance to be saved.

"Please be patient and be kind to one another as some of you are more adaptable than others. We are sending you great love, but we understand that what is going on now and will continue to go on may cause drastic changes for some that make you temporarily unhappy. If society here had not been so out of whack, there would not be a need for such drastic alterations of life as you knew it.

"What we are doing is for the common good of all, which some of you have trouble accepting. It has been a rather "it's-all-about-me" attitude here, and that is never a good thing. Not everywhere on the planet, but the United States in particular.

"You don't agree about much---that's evident. It's okay to have differences of opinion and question things. You'll learn the most with an open mind and when you are willing to listen to others. You will never have a religious experience like this one we are all having together at this miraculous time to make your world a peaceful and loving planet. It's magical, what you are witnessing.

"You know that was our intention. And you also know this planet is anything but a peaceful and loving planet right now, but hey, we are here to remedy that. We would hope most of you are happy to see some improvements happening. Health and happiness are yours.

"We need to talk more about food. So, what is the difference between food and chemical food? We make food, fruits and vegetables, grains, seeds. Animal meat is not something you must eat daily. It should be regarded as a meal enhancer on occasion and not the main item every meal. The obsession with meat is another marketing success that made corporations more money and made people unhealthier. The meat and dairy industries have not been taking your health into consideration. This is really a case of the United States of Greed.

"Remember the Native Americans? When they had meat to eat, they celebrated. They also had to hunt and slaughter their own deer, buffalo and other animals. One thing that made our hearts smile was how they always gave thanks to the animal for giving up its life so that they might be nourished. But they used every part of the animal, not just the meat. The hides were used, the bones were used and very little went to waste.

"How does that compare today? Can you even relate? Here is something you seniors may know about. Not that long ago Sunday dinners were special because of the roast chicken or pot roast being served. The week prior it was leftovers from the previous Sunday and many vegetables or casseroles until the next Sunday meat fest. It was simpler back then in the days before the meat and dairy industries began their campaigns to get you to eat more of their products. And of course, you did. Their advertising and promotions were so tantalizing many of you forgot that food is medicine. It never helped that the AMA didn't educate their doctors with any food-related education and the ADA endorsed anything they were paid to endorse. All of this will be corrected, and everyone given a true education on what really matters. You'll see a distinct drop in ailments and health improving.

"You will be going back in time with food. Meat will become less available with the CAFO's (concentrated animal feeding operations) being eliminated. On the bright side, farms that were on the brink of going under won't, and there will be a resurgence in people wanting to farm again. Farming is important and it will see a much deserved and respectful resurgence. While we are always proud to see progress on Earth, some things that you think are progress really are not at all. After seeing the live shots yesterday from the CAFO's, weren't you the least bit sick knowing that is the meat you buy at the stores?"

Logan was amused at the thought of going back in time with meals and not eating meat daily. Patti was talking about that last week. She had wondered if Logan realized how many meals, she was preparing had no meat in them. She was such a good cook that every meal was a treat. He pictured her listening to this at home and knew she would totally go along with this.

Gene Morrison, a cattle farmer in Wisconsin, was on the brink of bankruptcy. The meatpacking industry, in large part controlled by four major multinational companies who controlled some 85% of the business was also controlling prices. Ranchers like Gene were paid less for their cattle, but the packers charged the public more, thereby making huge profits at the expense of the ranchers. The ranchers were going out of business consequently, and most of the people thought the farmers/ranchers were the ones controlling the price of meat in the market.

To really screw the ranchers, packers went to Canada to buy cattle in 2020. Gene had to keep feeding the cattle he had though they were ready for market. It was an expense few ranchers could bear.

As Gene listened to the broadcast, he was praying that the reorganization that was imminent would save his ranch. Clearly there was dysfunction in the current system. He and his family listened to the broadcast with hope.

The broadcast continued.

"Consider the size of your super food stores. The cereal aisle can be thirty feet long or more. The majority of those boxes contain as much sugar as a candy bar. You have been so manipulated into thinking it is okay to eat anything in a box called breakfast cereal. You eat that sugar-laden stuff, worse yet you feed it to your children, and everyone is off to a sugar start.

"This is the worst thing you can do for your health. It is the same thing with the yogurt aisle, by the way. Add the fruit, or peanut butter or whatever "stuff" they add to yogurt, and you have fifteen new brands and flavors, fourteen of which should not even be there from a nutritional standpoint. We have removed everything and anything from your stores that is unhealthy. Factories manufacturing this will be undergoing their own makeovers. Only health-promoting choices will appear on the shelves from now on. Food manufacturing will be a huge makeover with all the unhealthy packaged food being eliminated.

"We spoke about sugar. Your government has been subsidizing the sugar industry. Your 'natural' experts tell you sugar is bad for you, which is very true. It fuels bacteria. It fuels cancer, causes cavities, and weight gain. There is sugar in most processed foods, which are really chemical foods at this point, devoid of natural goodness and nutrition. You can color them gone!

"The mere fact that the government has been helping the sugar industry out, while sugar is simultaneously causing ill health is a wonderment to us and it will end now. You want sweet? Try our fruits---they're delicious. Oh my people, stop screaming about chocolate, will you? Karen, especially you, sweetheart. We are not eliminating all sugar and certainly not chocolate with all of its good antioxidants. Dark chocolate has less sugar and it's the bomb as far as we are concerned.

"A video will be on the screens later today. Please watch *"How Not to Die"* by Dr. Michael Greger, which you can access on your YouTube any time, and it is available in book form as well. Please get truly involved in your health and what you are putting inside your bodies. It will help you now that the junk is out of the stores. You will shop smartly and get the nutrients you need for good health.

"Collectively you have not understood GMOs, and some of you just don't care about it. We are here to tell you; Jeffrey Smith is your expert writing *"Seeds of Deception"* and *"Genetic Roulette"*. This issue is mainly in your country because most of the EU, Turkey, Kyrgyzstan, Bhytan, Saudi Arabia, 43 countries in Africa, Peru, Ecuador, Venezuela and Belize have all banned GMOs. They paid attention to the researchers and will not allow GMO foods in their countries.

"How is it that your country, one that patriots hail as the greatest country on Earth, is so backwards? Why is there no global consensus? Why does the United States stand out as the leader of so many bad habits, bad food, and a people that are suffering from a good case of we-don't-care? Europeans have done a much better job working for their people and it's unfortunate that the U.S. so arrogantly thinks it is the best in the world at everything! You have more work to do in this country than almost any other country on the planet. In many countries it's just the government that needs reorganizing. In the United States it's just about everything, due to the government being in bed with corporations breeding greed.

"Jeffrey Smith's message is to stop buying food (chemical foods) with GMOs and they will stop making them because they will lose too much money, the idea being money talks. That doesn't seem to be working too well in your country where there is too much apathy, but if you follow the money, you'll see why."

Logan whispered to Jessie "The idea of a global consensus on anything would be astonishing, wouldn't it?"

Jessie nodded. She had been a vegetarian for years and the pictures of the CAFO's made her sick to her stomach. Her ex-husband was a strict carnivore and the battles over her attempts to cut back on the amount of meat he consumed were ridiculous. She would make meat for him, only eating the vegetables herself, but he would rage at her for being a hippy. There were other disagreements besides the meat issue which led to them going their separate ways.

During the pauses in broadcasting, Jessie and Logan could hear the construction going on down the corridor from their offices. It wouldn't be long until they would be packing up. And going where? Nobody knew yet. It was a bit unsettling, but neither Logan nor Jessie was worried. There was an unspoken sense of relief shared between them. A new chapter was beginning for everyone and everything and there was something adventurous about it, rather than it being worrisome.

The God Center continued.

"To us, once again, massive profits being made for some while the people eating their adulterated foods get sick. For the naysayers, the cumulative poisons in GMOs when consumed regularly do cause disease but because it occurs on a cumulative basis and you don't drop dead instantly eating GMO corn, 'they' claim it's harmless. We have come from the God Center to tell you truths. GMOs are being eliminated. We are disappointed that marketing won over science yet again. Money talks too much in the U.S. - period. And processed foods may be convenient, have longer shelf life and are cheaper but the added sugar, salt and chemicals greatly contribute to disease. They will be changed or eliminated.

"We see the statistics. 42% are obese. Interesting that in 1950 it was only 10%. We are concerned that you are not taking your health seriously enough and are falling prey to marketing and those chemists who labor to make you addicted to junk. We have eliminated all 'diet' foods and beverages. They are a joke. Eat real food, the food we make, not the food created in laboratories. We'll admit we had to try eating a marshmallow yesterday out of sheer curiosity. Air and sugar it is. So, when we saw that some cereal manufacturers put marshmallows in the cereal, well, can you imagine our collective outrage?

"We do sort of apologize to the 42 percent of you who are obese, and the borderline group of seriously overweight. You know who you are. You get a lot of flak for your weight which drives some of you to eat more for some reason.

"Here's the thing, we are here to help you even though you don't think we are. It is critical that you understand everything being done here is not to punish you but because the God Center truly loves you. Chemical foods of all kinds are disappearing, just like the drugs. You may experience going 'cold turkey' but we must do this for the well-being of your personal health and that of the Earth. Internal organs cannot function when they are being snuffed out, seriously choked to the brink of dysfunction, by your fat. With the obesity rates so high, chair manufacturers made bigger chairs! No! Stop that. You are catering to the people on self-destruct, and people, OMP, listen to the God

Center! Eat real food. This concludes our broadcast on food. We will give you time to digest this."

Realizing the country was not under attack, despite the silver-pod grid above the Earth, allowed people in some areas to resume their daily activities. But the pods and messages were all anyone was talking about.

"The God Center? Really? You think this is really God?" Stan asked. He and his friend Pete were sitting in the bar called Nowhere Else. It was smokey in the bar even though smoking had been prohibited. Considering what was going on, even former smokers lit up with the thought of life as they knew it disappearing.

"I don't know that it's God. How would I know? But I will say that the voice is telling us we couldn't clean up the Earth or ourselves and now they've come to do it for us," Pete replied.

"Sure, Pete, what about our freedoms, huh? Some silver pods come to change everything without fucking asking if we want to change. Well, I don't want to!" Stan snapped.

"You know you have the opportunity to raise your hand and be removed. You want that? I saw Mrs. Bracone put her hand up yesterday, and poof she was gone!" Pete replied.

"She was old, and she missed her dead husband. Who cares if the old people leave?"

"Wow, Stan. I never realized how negative you are, and mean too," Pete said, shaking his head in disbelief. They had been friends since college. They both worked in media which was undergoing enormous change.

There were many like Stan, having this attitude about the changes. Likewise, many like Pete were being open minded, if not optimistic.

Attitudes varied; the God Center noted. From time-to-time brief personal messages were sent to individuals who were struggling. The God center was patient and loving, but the love came across as tough love and there was some resistance, which was expected.

"Oh God, how am I going to pay my bills?" moaned Beth Mason, morning anchor on Memphis TV.

"You'll be back to work next week, dear Beth," the God Center offered her consolation.

"You aren't eliminating the media?"

"We thought it best to suspend it while we are busy working out the changes. You see we are using it to inform and teach our children. So many have been living without the knowledge of many things, while others may know about it but do not think it's important, or that it applies to them, so they discount it.

"But the news, well, it is very frustrating to see such polarized news, depending on who you watch. We are giving people time to realize that reporting the news has evolved into over analyzing, and major misrepresentations of truth. We want truth in reporting," replied the God Center. "Giving opinions will not change facts, so just the facts now."

"I can't believe we are getting raises, like double our salary!" Connie chirped happily. She had worked at Holy Family Hospital as a nurse for twelve years. The nurse's lounge wasn't as ornately decorated as the rest of the hospital. There was one sofa, its brown fabric worn from years of use. There were four round tables with cheap Formica tops and around each table four molded plastic chairs. In order to take a desperately needed break, the only way to put your feet up was to sit on the sofa and grab a chair to put your feet up. Besides the coffeemaker and a small refrigerator, the lounge was uncomfortably Spartan.

"I'll believe it when I see it." was the dour reply from Nell. "Nurses always get told they should be paid more, but it never happens." Nell was seated on the sofa rubbing her sore knees from a long day of endless floor runs.

"You've got that wrong. Wayne Dyer wrote the opposite. He says, 'You'll see it when you believe it.' But also this is the God Center telling us! I don't think that grid of silver space discs, or whatever they are, is here just to take pictures!" Connie replied.

"It's kind of freaky though, don't you think? I mean you can look out any window and see those silver things just hovering over us. I am trying to be okay with it, but I'm not," Nell said.

"We hear you," said the God Center, "changes being made will benefit everyone but most importantly will save you and the planet. Be patient. We love you, Nell.

"Holy crap, they heard!" Nell said shocked. "I guess I should watch what I say."

At the Chevy dealership, a meeting of the minds was occurring. There were many conversations going on everywhere that had two opposing views.

"I knew it would come to this. This is the second coming! Be ready to repent," Gary told Frank. Gary was raised in the Baptist church. Anytime anyone had a problem, Gary would quote scripture in an effort to help them. It seemed he memorized just enough to drive away people, especially those who were not biblically inclined.

"Oh my God, Gary! Seriously? You Bible bangers! I do believe this is the first and only coming. They could have just blown up this planet.

They said so! No, it's not repentance. It's an opportunity to have Earth be a place for all to thrive and be happy. You watch! They are going to level the playing field alright. I hope those billionaires having their little space races get their money taken away and reallocated. How about that God Center?" He smirked.

Hearing the question, the reply from the God Center was instant.

"Do we plan on reallocating? It's done already. We did that last night while you all were sleeping. You may be surprised to learn that their money is helping in several of your more critical areas of neglect. We are in the process of fixing the veterans crisis you all talk about yet do nothing. We have teams in the major cities finding homes for the homeless. Have you seen Portland or Los Angeles? The stories we are hearing from those we are finding homes for would break your heart because it sure breaks our hearts. Yes, good to have the funds to fix this.

"Oh, and Gary? Frank is correct. We haven't been here since creation, but we've watched you, we sent help via messengers. And believe us---we had no intention of coming back here. We set up planets with living organisms, not always human as you are, and we observe our creations. Everything we create is a part of us. We never wanted things to evolve into mayhem here!

"You have missed the messages we sent through so many wonderful people! Gary, here's one for you. You like Jimi Hendrix. He said, we are quoting ourselves here indirectly, 'When the power of love overcomes the love of power, the world will know peace.' How's that message? Mahatma Gandhi said it too, but Jimi put it to music."

"Are you telling me that Jimi Hendrix was one of your messengers?" Gary asked, with eye-popping innocence. "Incredible!" He shook his head in amazement.

"We use people all the time, in bits and pieces. We don't have as many full-time messengers as we do the surprise part-timers. We've sent messages through hundreds and hundreds of people. Some messages are subtle but sourced from us nonetheless."

Gary's curiosity was piqued. "Oh yeah? Who else?"

"Ram Dass had a beautiful message. Know him? He said 'All I am is loving awareness. I am loving awareness. It means that wherever I look, anything that touches my awareness will be loved by me.' Spot on! Try using that as a guide and see how much love can be in your life."

"Wasn't he the guy that did LSD and crazy drugs?"

"He did. People do crazy things, nobody is perfect, but he had so much potential, and he studied with people who led him to a beautiful state of peace and love. We felt he served messaging well. And Gary? Don't be obsessed with perfection. Leave perfection to the Divine. That's us. When humans have their moments of perfection, and many, many do, it is because we helped them achieve it. But these are momentary blips of perfection. No human is perfect 100 percent of the time. That is our job."

People everywhere were either on edge, confused, scared or jubilant at this time. It was an emotional smorgasbord. There were combinations of fear that flipped into joy or vice versa. People had been instructed to go about their daily lives, observing and listening to broadcasts when they came on. This was not limited to the United States. Broadcasts were going on all over the world.

In Italy, for example, the Vatican was being emptied of its people and treasure. People there, the pope included were assigned housing in the many monasteries in the country. Italy's debt is the highest level in over a century. It was not sustainable without intervention and the Catholics would never dream of touching the Vatican, which is considered to be the wealthiest 'country' per capita in the world and estimates of it's worth are in excess of fifteen billion. Italy kept borrowing money, much like the United States, digging its debt hole deeper. The God Center knew the world's population of Catholics were in for a major shock, but the whole of the country would be better served by using the Vatican money to set their economy right again. The money necessary to run this religion can be used elsewhere.

Representatives from the God Center went through the Top Secret chambers, through volumes in 53 miles of shelving, more than 35,000 volumes of catalog. There are twelve centuries worth of documents. Much would be made public and that struck terror in the hearts of those who only suspected what was in the volumes but dared not ask.

In South America, many countries like Columbia have drug cartels producing an estimated 70% of the world's cocaine. Columbia is the third most populated country in South America, five times the size of the United Kingdom. Farmers there have been trying desperately to plant other crops such as melon, black pepper, pineapple and yucca to export instead of cocaine. It was also to feed the countries hungry. They are receiving help from the God Center there. The cocaine has been eliminated.

Life was changing globally. It rained in the western states like California and Nevada, where dried up rivers and lakes started to fill. It rained in Moldova and the Ukraine where severe droughts are all too common. Australia, so desperate for water that cities like Melbourne, Sydney and Perth built desalination plants in an effort to partially drought-proof themselves, also received a truly God-sent rain. Northern India, Spain, Syria and parts of Brazil were all suffering drought but now are receiving gentle daily rains that would soon fill reservoirs and crops would grow once more to feed the people.

Everyone near a media screen could see the changes for themselves. In that respect, the God Center didn't just talk about what was going on, it showed the people. Scenes from across the globe were being shown on the screens everywhere, on phones, computers and televisions.

The God Center knew it would take seeing the global changes to accept the reality of what they were hearing about. Even with that, there are the crazies that deny it, thinking its fake news or some conspiracy of who knows what. Many were so adamant about their beliefs that their elimination was a distinct possibility. The God Center would allow everyone a second chance, and is forgiving, understanding and loving. All of that has its limits.

There are laboratories across the globe doing scientific research. The God Center addressed each one. Any lab working on chemical warfare, poisons, viruses that could kill were immediately cleared of anything destructive. The researchers would be given new assignments or retrained to produce immune boosting serums to save lives rather than destroy them. Any laboratory doing research to produce new drugs were likewise halted until they could be retrofitted with other life enhancing programs.

Jason Thackery in Melbourne stood at the edge of his property watching the nearby fields get greener in the one day of gentle rains they were experiencing. "Thank you, God! We've prayed for rain for so long. We thought you'd forgotten us." he said out loud to himself.

Hearing this, the God Center replied in an instant. "We did hear your prayers. There were terrible conditions on this planet because of drought in some places, floods in others. We are here to get things in order, and we did not forget about you folks 'down under'."

Jason was surprised at the immediate response. "Wow, you heard me?"

"We miss nothing. Unfortunately, right now we have a planet of some confused and still fearful people, but we are delighted to see our changes have already brought happiness to you. There could be quite a few people leaving this week, rather than going through change. We are re-booting Earth as well as the people. Keep up your kindness, and attitude of cooperation. All is well. We love you!"

Sandova in Brazil was on his knees in his field, in the rain, praising God. It was happening all over the globe, farmers elated and full of hope. It seemed that the majority, globally speaking, were deliriously happy with the changes, mostly the rain of course because that meant not starving. But in the United States it was apparent who the spoiled child in the bunch was.

The head of the largest computer company had been one of the wealthiest men in the world. Had been. His fortune was now being used for critical infrastructure needed on roads and bridges. He had considered himself quite the philanthropist in the past. Now he really earned that distinction, albeit not entirely voluntarily.

A similar observation showed a slightly upset woman, a TV mogul, bemoaning the fact that she was only allowed to keep two of her seven homes. Her fortune now provided temporary decent housing for immigrants, temporary schools to teach English and job-training programs for immigrants. Then, with millions left over, scholarships were created for trade schools.

Rebuilding this economy and bringing jobs back to the United States from overseas meant workers would be needed for all the factory and tech jobs. There would be some money used for building businesses that offer repairs on vehicles, appliances, and homes with general services. It was a massive benefit to humanity and the economy. To appease the egos of some of the wealthiest 'contributors' their names would appear on the new buildings, bridges and wherever their fortunes went for the benefit of all.

The super-wealthy would never have given up their fortunes without this intervention. Oh, sure they made 'contributions' but what the God Center wanted--- demanded---was a leveling of the playing field. And it was being done everywhere on Earth. The God Center did not discriminate. The God Center created humanity with diversity so the observation of it wouldn't be boring. There was more than enough money to go around with 22 million millionaires and 1,000 billionaires. There would be no more starving people on this planet. There would be no person denied health care nor would there ever be a family going bankrupt over medical bills. National debt was a thing of the past.

When Logan arrived at his office in the Pentagon, there was a lot of commotion in the corridor adjacent to his. He and Jessie watched the broadcast together, knowing their tenure there was coming to an end.

When the broadcast was over, she went down the hall to the lady's room. It was being torn apart but the workers allowed her to use the facilities, warning her that she needed to evacuate. She ran back to the office to tell Logan. "We're being evacuated now," Jessie said replying to the expression on Logan's face and the raised eyebrow.

"Okay, where to?" he asked.

"We haven't been told that yet. We're just to pack up and go home for now. We will be contacted where to go when all this rearranging is complete. At least that's what the angels said," she replied.

"Angels?" Logan queried.

"That's what they are Logan. They are representatives but honestly, look at them. All white and sort of glowing. They're angels, besides if they work for God, what else would you call them?"

"Hmm, hadn't thought of it, but okay. Angels it is. Where's Manuel, have you talked to him?" Logan asked her.

"He couldn't come in today so we will have to pack his personal belongings. I called him to find out if I had everything, he wanted packed in his box. I guess he had quite the evening with Maria, the kids, and her whole family. How did it go with Patti?"

"Probably a lot better than it went for Manuel. Patti burned her Bible this morning in the fireplace. She was in pieces last night, but I think Matt helped her more than I did.

"Patti hates lies, so he reminded her of that. Let's face it, she has been duped like millions of others, if not outright lied to and I think she's kinda pissed about it now. Better pissed than all hysterical I figure," Logan said as he was taking personal belongings out of his desk drawers and the pictures of his family off of his credenza. Looking at the family portrait taken several years ago, he smiled at it. That photo was taken on vacation in St. Lucia. He remembered it well and longed to return. His thoughts about the wonderful time in St. Lucia were interrupted.

"What about our research papers? What about the top secrets reports? What do we do with this stuff? We aren't supposed to leave this are we?" Jessie asked.

"Ha, it's all garbage now kiddo! It will be interesting to see where we end up when all of this rearranging is done. Just take what is personally yours. They'll be tearing these offices apart for the renovation anyway. Doubtful our research on UAP's holds any value whatsoever at this point. Our jobs are obsolete now. Wow, what a day can bring, huh?" Logan said.

"Wow, you're right Logan. What the hell was I thinking anyway? I'm curious about our jobs going forward. I must work; we need the money. Chelsea can't pay the rent on her salary alone," Jessie confessed.

"I'm sure everything will work out okay." Logan said as he continued to purge through his drawers. "Like I told Patti, change had to happen. Better it should be a God-supervised change than setting off nukes annihilating everything and everyone or whatever damn disaster would be heading our way."

"Oh, I wish I was that confident, Logan," Jessie replied.

"Think of it as a vacation for now. If leveling the playing field regarding money is concerned, I'm sure you'll be fine. Assuming this is a total makeover, and let's face it, does God do things half-assed? No. So you'll probably have a substantial decrease in the exorbitant amount of rent you're paying now anyway," Logan said, taping up the box of his personal belongings. "Funny this is all I have that's exclusively mine after all the years I've been here. One box. One box and I'm outta here!" Logan said smiling.

"Keep in touch, Logan! I sure hope you're right about the finances. We'll see. I may be on your doorstep, suitcase in hand otherwise," she said teasingly, and gave her co-worker a big hug.

"Jessie, why don't you and Chelsea come to dinner tonight? Frankly I think a lot of your knowledge of ancient cultures might help Patti handle things better," Logan added. "She loves research. This would give her something to get involved with besides burning her religious books."

"Sounds good. I can bring some books for her too if you would like," Jessie said. "She better not burn them!" she added laughing.

"Perfect! See you about 6?" he asked.

"I'll be there. Not sure about Chelsea but I'll come for sure. Thanks Logan. I sure hope we can continue to work together, wherever we end up."

As this day was coming to a close with much done and more to go the God Center made another broadcast globally.

"We have been questioned many times today about who our messengers have been over time. Can you not sense for yourself when someone is speaking or writing pure God Center material? Have you been so blinded by your organized religions and their silly dogma, that you discount words from anyone else besides your priest, or reverend or rabbi? There are many of you---I will use Marie as an example---she reads only books on religion by Catholic authors. What a small window! There is so much else out there. If you had all really studied your history instead of hiding in your bubbles, things that will blow your mind going forward would not come as a shock at all.

"The Bible people bless your hearts. Let me just say this: better messaging in spirituality. Oh my people, you will find messages everywhere, in music, books or lectures on videos and listen to them. When we leave, the messages will still be here. Let them comfort you if needed. We have revealed some in our broadcasts.

"Your scientists and archaeologists discounted what they unearthed and saw in ancient cultures as mythology. It had to be myths because their findings seemed impossible. The pictures on cave walls and on stones were considered stories from a primitive culture and not the recordings of their history. Your Earth received engineering, mathematics, and physics thousands of years ago from the 'sky gods', which was what the ancients believed their 'visitors' were. That knowledge was given across the globe, everywhere. Archaeologists and historians have looked within cultures but never across the cultures. Pertinent questions were unanswered as a result.

"They have been studying this for over a century but still, nobody wants to believe what was found. We will show you before we leave that what you refer to as 'aliens' were indeed here, and they did much to advance your world. Your ancient history experts knew what they saw, they just didn't believe it either.

"There was a fear of truthfully sharing lest the careers of those archaeologists and scientists blow up with global laughter. That would have been led by the churches because it wrecks every creation story you made up for yourselves. We put all your diverse races on this planet and sent you 'sky gods' if you will, from other planets to advance your culture. Do think about this.

"And speaking of thinking, did you know that we can see when you are thinking? A section of your brain lights up when you are thinking, and we can see this though you cannot. You should have seen the glowing brains when we first got here yesterday. It was like Las Vegas lights in your heads. Every one of you, lit up like the Fourth of July, we swear. Ordinarily though, we see mere candles flickering here and there, like one would during a power outage. Yes. It is that bad, you're thinking or not thinking as is the case. As you are shown the global changes, we see a lot of lit up brains. Change will do that."

The faculty lounge at Evanston High School was filled to capacity with the staff listening to the God Center. Students had been sent home, but the teachers lingered well past the last bell.

"This is unbelievable! We are witnessing the biggest shift of mankind directed by none other than God," whispered Mr. Henry, chemistry teacher, to his favorite teacher of all, Miss Geyer. She reached for his hand and squeezed it, her silent acknowledgment. The two had been dating secretly and had planned a summer wedding. She leaned over toward Mr. Henry to whisper back close to his ear, "Shh, I want to hear every word."

"Can we dust off your brains? We gave you all good brains. Why are so few using them? You could start by feeding them well. Ten walnuts a day is phenomenal brain food. And weren't we oh so clever? Walnuts cut open look just like your brain. See? We were giving you instructions without even saying a word. Brains need good fats and water. Hey, get away from the potato chips. They are fat alright but not good fat. Better to eat avocados, fatty fish, blueberries, broccoli, pumpkin seeds or hooray for dark chocolate. Did you see potato chips on this list? No. Use your brain. And assuming you are using your brain, have you noticed anything about the foods listed above? Did they come from a factory or did the God Center make them?

"We heard doctors and scientists over the last 30-40 years discussing the dumbing down of America. Think they're crazy? They are not. This is just another reason to save you all. Jane Healy, a PhD, wrote a book in 1990 called *"Endangered Minds"* about why children don't think and what we can do about it. Brilliant work! Every parent and teacher should have this book as required reading.

"The curriculum in schools has been watered down over decades. Why? We are going to change the entire educational system. We are providing you with true history books for your schools, unbiased and full of truth. We are wondering how you will adjust to the truth, especially regarding religions, but your schools' educational programs? It is in sorry shape. And book burning? All of sudden you don't want your children exposed to all that is out there? You call this education?

"You have some awesome teachers across your country that will be getting their just rewards and they don't have to come to heaven to get them --- a little God humor there --- they will receive far more compensation.

"Why does a second grader need a calculator? Somehow making math easier by pressing buttons on a machine makes the brain sleep. So here are kids at that age and we don't want them to use their brains to do simple math? Multiplication tables used to be memorized. That was using brain power, not calculators. We do not understand why children are not being taught to think. They grow up into adults who can't make change at a store without seeing what the cash register says. No brain activity. That is a huge part of your society's problem. No brain activity and too much reliance on your technologies.

"How many books did you read this year? This month? There walk among you far too many people who never read. We've heard people bragging --- bragging --- about the fact that they haven't read a book in decades. Oh my people! It's the best exercise for your brain that we could ever give you. Picture this, if you will. We will make it a very simplified explanation.

"Draw an oval with a line down the center. This is your brain. Left of the line is the left brain, right brain is the other side of the line. When you watch television, which is a passive activity for your brain, there is a small squiggle of activity going from left to right up and down that dividing line. Now reading? You will see lines going from left to right almost to the outer edges of the oval. Reading stimulates your brain.

"Great brain exercise! Use it or lose it folks! We are serious so consider your Source, the God Center. We have much to do while you sleep so we will end our broadcast with a good night to you all."

"I don't like to read," Tiffany whined.

"I don't like to floss my teeth either, but it's good for me and I do it. You heard God, Tiffany. It is good for your brain," Len countered.

"It takes only minutes to floss, Leonard. It can take days to read a book."

"How much time do you spend shopping, Tiffany? How much time lunching with the girls, and getting your spa time in? You need time management and some time with no credit cards. That can be arranged, you know."

She sat pouting, feeling like a child whose toys had been taken away. Reading, she thought, was a total bore and leave it to Len to suggest boring things. At least he hadn't brought up having a baby again! Not yet anyway.

Len and Tiffany had celebrated their eighth anniversary last weekend. Len had taken Tiffany to dinner at a very expensive restaurant and had given her diamond stud earrings. She'd pouted. What Tiffany wanted was a European cruise. Len had suggested she go to work and save for the trip. It had been an ugly scene in the restaurant that evening, and it gave Len more doubts than he already had for this marriage. He wanted children, a family. Tiffany wasn't at all interested in sharing Len's desires. Only his money it appeared. With all the changes in the air, there could be one more for him only on a very personal level.

"It was hard at school today. The kids are very distracted and hyped up over all this. They call it the God Invasion. Mostly I think they're excited about it," Marge told her husband Bill.

"Nobody is getting work done at my office either. Everyone is speculating about what it will be like when the God Center finishes cleaning up our world. I'd like to believe it will be peaceful, but I fear as soon as we are left to our own devices, it will get crazy again," Bill mused.

"I think the bad seeds will be eliminated, or 'removed' as the God Center puts it. Barb at work said she thinks God is a communist," Marge replied, chuckling.

"I'm sure God would not like those labels. You know labeling people is a judgment?" he asked.

"I never considered that, but you're probably right."

"I've always believed that we were created in the image of God. I just wish we could actually see him!" Len said.

The God Center intervened. "Len, you can see God everywhere. We are in all things, believe it or not, so everywhere you go, you go with God in you and in all that you see. Even when you are looking at something that man/woman created, it was the God in them that did the creating."

"Oh my God, you heard me?"

"Yes, we miss nothing, even your thoughts. Don't let that creep you out. It's for your own good. Think of me as a father listening to his children, because that is what this is, isn't it? We hear from some that the God Center is harsh and perhaps dictatorial, oh and Marge? Tell Barb we are certainly not communist. There is so much to correct on this planet, it may seem radical, but there you have it. Calling names at God? Hmm, think about this."

"Well, I am glad you are here because we've felt for quite some time that the world was in a horrid mess. We were even trying to think of another country to move to, but it seemed there were problems everywhere. Hard to know what to do, ya know? But you're here and oh my God I am talking to God!" Len said, astonishing himself with the present reality.

Marge laughed, "Yeah Len, you're talking to God, and you haven't had a drink or drugs!"

"Len, my child, you can talk to us any time. No need to memorize prayers, as some of the religions tell you to. We tend to ignore those. We want to hear from your heart, not some memorized thing somebody else made up. So, get real and realize that you can access your source by speaking from the heart. We love to hear gratitude, reflections on all the good things, more than anything. Some people beg and carry on with their wants and needs. It's backwards. Acknowledging the good things produces more good. No need to tell us what you do not want we already know that. But your focus on what you don't want just produces more of that.

"Many have been told they are so stupidly optimistic about everything, as if that is a bad thing. It's not. Staying positive is an act of faith in the God Center. Remember that."

In Tennessee, Lisa Gunot was crying with her son Kenny in her arms.

"Mom, why can't we see who is in the silver space pods?" Kenny inquired.

"Because it is spirit energy according to the voice," mom Lisa replied, shaking and trying to hold it together.

"Is it really God in there?"

"I don't know. This is not how the Bible described Armageddon. And Jesus said many would come in His name to fool us."

"So you think it is evil then?"

"Anyone trying to tell me that Jesus was just a messenger and not our Savior, cannot be sent by God or play like they're God," Lisa replied weeping softly.

The God Center intervened.

"My dearest Lisa, your Armageddon, as you call it, is already here. It is being fought inside of you as you struggle with the forces of fear, self-doubt, apathy and ignorance within. First let us clarify, you are not ignorant, but you have been manipulated. We will explain.

"As for Jesus, yes, he was the son of God. Kenny is the son of God too. So you are a child of God, Lisa. All humans on this planet are sons and daughters of God. Start accepting this first. The true history of Jesus and his teachings is so important. He was on a mission for the God Center on Earth.

"Jesus denounced the ruling classes, not just the wealthy and powerful but even the religious authorities for their exploitation and oppression of people in their lands. He wanted a level playing field. He rejected the subservient and separate position of women and befriended women, which was considered heresy. He was a dangerous revolutionary, too radical for the androcratic, or male dominated, society.

"Jesus was sent to you because we wanted a cultural transformation for all of humanity. That was the message we sent him with from the

God Center. He rejected the dogma that priests, nobles and kings are God's favorites, and he never preached that women are spiritually inferior. He recognized that your spiritual evolution was being prohibited by the power systems in charge, but the systems resistance at that time was too strong.

"In the New Testament, his intended liberation of women and the true simple teachings of Jesus were smothered or complicated and misconstrued on purpose. The contradictory dogma packaged in your Bible was put there on purpose to justify the church's androcratic structure and goals.

"By contrast, Jesus preached the gospel of a partnership society. His revolution of nonviolence ended up with his brutal death on a cross. Early Christians who would not knuckle under and accept the dogma of the male dominated society were in trouble. What followed much later was the savagery of their 'holy' Crusades, their witch hunts, burning books and people.

"How could anyone believe they were trying to spread the love of Jesus and therefore their mandates were justified? They wanted to 'appear' to be carrying out the work of Jesus. But, in fact, they were creating a stronghold, a stranglehold, on anyone who would not bend under their commands using church rule. Killing in the name of religion is still killing though the church colored it as a religious duty? So, then it's okay? No, it is never okay to kill.

"The manipulated writings that are included in your Bible make you think it was Jesus-based, but in truth they only wanted to keep the androcratic systems in place. These systems, both political and social, are male dominated just as the churches wanted it to be for control.

"You grew up with the Bible as your guidebook for life. That is not a bad thing, it's just wrong. There are many biblical scholars who have given their lives to study and authenticate those writings. Have you ever read what the scholars have discovered? Errors, contradictions, political intent, and thousands of manuscripts left out intentionally. There was much disagreement among them about what verses and even what books should be contained in the Bible, and how those verses read. Very clever orchestration!

"Eliminated from any inclusion in their bible book were all the women who wrote prolifically, many of whom were leaders in the Christian movement after the crucifixion. They only included just enough about Jesus to make you believe all the packaging they wrote around him to retain control of their male dominated systems. You will learn more when the Vatican documents are all made public.

"My child, and please know that you are my child, we have been sending messengers with clear and simple to understand messages, for instance, Moses. We sent the Ten Commandments, simple. Jesus was a beacon of light with messages on other planets, so we sent him here too. His core message was (drum roll please) the Kingdom of God. He gave the Sermon on the Mount where he prioritized for you with *'But seek first the Kingdom of God and His righteousness, and all these things shall be added to you.'* He told you about the primary purpose for his life was to give you this message. He taught love, compassion, honesty, non-judgment, and joy.

"He messaged very well for us, the God Center, or Kingdom of God which was the former name humans gave us. Yours was not the only planet we sent him to. He was in four other galaxies before he came to Earth. His messages were very well received elsewhere and did much to encourage the inhabitants of other planets to be 'as one', to love, share, to help each other. But on Earth? While some of the people loved him, those in power did not and they eliminated any chance that a peaceful partnership society would ever exist.

"All the instructions Jesus gave on his other missions enabled the inhabitants on other planets to progress by leaps and bounds. Looking at their accelerated lineup of priorities, accounts for the outstanding contrast with you on Earth. His contribution on our other locations is obvious as you will soon see for yourself.

"He came to Earth, but it was already too greedy, too political, with power hungry leadership. Retaining dominance, male dominated of course, was the one focus. The leaders made the mistake of making Jesus into a martyr and so the fiction stories began. Perhaps knowing this will make you more receptive?

"He was your teacher, not your savior. He told you that, many times but it was Paul and others who created that Savior story. The teachings were very simple and basic. So, we are the one doing the saving, not him. That was never his assignment. The God Center is here now to save humanity and the planet. And Lisa, we are the only one that can save anything.

"However, Jesus wasn't the only messenger. Your history has clouded up, confused, and distorted everything to the point that some people are condemning others for 'not believing' in an inaccurate book, your Bible. This is yet another reason we came here. Let's clear up all your tragic misunderstandings.

"We have come to tell you all, all our precious children that you were made with a God Center in your heart. We love you so much we want you to know that we are intimately connected. Whenever you have love, compassion, honesty, non-judgment and joy in your heart, you are on our channel, just like your radios, dial us in. It's simple, not confusing or even open to interpretation."

Lisa sat quietly listening, while she held on to Kenny tightly. Tears streamed down her face. Her heart was pounding, beads of sweat on her forehead.

"It's not what I was taught my whole life!" she mumbled rather angrily; her confusion vocalized.

"We understand. But Lisa, you were taught love, compassion and honesty. You did get the message. You simply had a package around it, the Jesus story. You don't need the package, but you really need what is inside of it. We have been amused that humans on this planet complicate the simplest things. It's like watching children color. You over-color, putting layers and layers of colors on top of one another until you lose the outline of what you're coloring.

"Do you understand? Humans created thousands of man-made religions, with intentions that are varied as your zoo animals. It did nothing but divide humanity up into pieces, rather than unite everyone. This world of yours has racial prejudice, religious prejudice and sexual prejudice. Do you honestly think that God wants to see that kind of division, let alone all the persecution that stems from it? We are here to unify and clearly spell out for you what love and compassion should be!"

"Mom don't cry. I know everything will be okay. If they were going to kill us, they would have by now," Kenny said as he tried to pry himself from Lisa's grip. Kenny, at ten years old, was maturing right in front of his mother. He sat up tall and patted her shoulder to comfort her.

"Oh Kenny, you are so much like your father. He would have said the same thing. And the fact that you are so brave, I just wish your father had lived to see this!"

The God Center heard every word and thought everywhere and could communicate simultaneously with individuals as they desired to or used the broadcasts for mass messaging. There were conversations going on between clergy, doctors, teachers, whoever desired communication from the God Center. When the media resumed, the fact that the messaging was consistent everywhere on the globe was astounding to the most seasoned reporters. They were used to politicians, who were the best at mixed-messaging and frankly, bullshitting.

"Hi honey, I'm home," Logan said as he came through the door with his box of personal items.

Patti was shocked. It was too early for Logan to be home, she hurried to the front door. "What happened? Oh no, is that box from work? Were you fired or what?" she said giving him a kiss on the cheek. "Come into the kitchen and tell me all about what is going on I'm just starting dinner."

After Logan put the box on his desk in the den, he entered the kitchen. "Patti, I hope you don't mind but I invited Jess and her roommate for dinner tonight."

"Good thing I'll have enough food. Matt is coming too. It'll be a party I guess," she said cheerfully. "I had a long talk with my parents today. They said everything is quiet out in California, except for a large contingent of hippies rallying in the streets positively jubilant. Mom and dad are okay and feeling pretty optimistic about the future now. I think dad is now convinced he won't have to move out of the country because of the political craziness. You know he was serious about that."

"They asked about you and your job and wanted to know what was going on at the Pentagon – although they saw on the screens that the renovation was already going on. I told them we weren't sure where you would be assigned when everything is restructured. Dad said we could come out for a visit. Wouldn't that be something to consider since you are temporarily out of work?" she asked.

"Guess so. I may be around the house awhile until things get sorted out. The Pentagon is getting renovated into apartments, many departments are being eliminated altogether so I have no idea at this point where the hell I'll fit into the big plan," Logan said, pouring himself a drink.

"I'd say it's too early for that drink, but maybe not! This is all rather unsettling, isn't it?" she said while chopping onions. "Pour one for me too, please."

"It's a makeover, no doubt about that! I'm flabbergasted this is all moving so quickly. I'm used to the government pace which sometimes doesn't move at all," he said, sipping his scotch. Logan was relieved that at least Patti's spirits had improved and having Matt come for dinner was always something she enjoyed. He wasn't sure that Patti was okay. She could be just putting on a brave front, but he thought tonight was better than last and maybe that's how it will go.

Patti worked as a free-lance writer from home. "Well, this all certainly gives me fodder for writing, doesn't it?" she mused. "I've been making lists of topics to pursue but its best I wait for a bit to write an article. I've been writing volumes in my journal though."

"Good Patti! I know journaling is good for you and I might start my own journal since I'm home in this state of suspension. This time at home will also give me time to do a few projects around the house. Got any?" Logan asked.

"Are you kidding? Of course," Patti laughed.

Three years his junior, Patti was the perfect match for Logan. She grew up in Berkeley, California as an only child. Her father, a molecular biology professor at the University, passed on his love of science to his daughter. Her mother, a botanist at the University's Botanical Garden, passed on to Patti a reverence for plants and gardening. It showed up in the landscape of the Georgian she and Logan bought. The backyard was a replica of an English garden, sculpted, colorful, and the envy of their neighborhood.

Patti attended Berkeley for two years and then transferred to Columbia University in New York for her degree in journalism. Patti loved the east coast and wanted to stay there after graduating, landing a job as a junior reporter at the New York Times. Her parents bought her a condo to live in because she didn't make enough money to afford rent in New York. She met Logan through mutual friends, and they knew in their hearts immediately, although it took several years before they married, that they were meant for each other.

The couple settled outside of Washington DC due to Logan's job at the Pentagon and Patti continued to work as a free-lance writer, while raising their two sons. The boys brought challenges but so much joy to the couple. They could serve as a 'poster' family. Typical conflicts but with love taking center stage, it had been a good life so far. There were many fun vacations, mostly to California so Patti could visit her parents. The children brought laughter and joy into their grandparent's lives.

"Well, bring on your honey do list m'lady and all will be done. I'll be happy to be kept busy now. You know how I can't just sit around waiting for I don't even know what," Logan said, with the reality of what he'd just said beginning to give him concern.

"Hey lovey," Patti replied. "Whatever comes we are in this together, ya know," she added as she put her arms around the love of her life and kissed him passionately.

Don't be trapped by dogma – which is
the result of other people's thinking.

Steve Jobs

DAY THREE

With the God Center's media coverage, people could see the miracles taking place simultaneously across the Earth. The rains where drought had lived, the crops growing, the parks and highways clean with no homeless tents, workers fixing highways and bridges, but most of all, there were no killings of human beings anywhere on the planet, no violence to show. For once all the 'news' appeared to be good news. So much was happening, critical changes that were so desperately needed that people were in awe of the transformations taking place.

In Chicago, the midtown police department phones were quieter, and many of the officers sat drinking coffee while the broadcasts were on. This type of quiet was exceptional. "I don't know what those pods are doing, Lieutenant, but our radios haven't received any calls of shootings or dead bodies being found in the last 48 hours," said the desk sergeant, "but domestic disturbances are keeping the fleet busy trying to calm people down."

"It's certainly remarkable for Chicago," Lieutenant Bristol exclaimed. "This must be God, especially if this continues one more day. This is just so unbelievable."

"Hey, you think that's unbelievable? Go downstairs and see the cache of weapons being turned in."

Conversations across the globe in all law enforcement offices were similar. Remarkably, no gun shots had been fired since the silver orb grid enveloped the planet, except by some drunks and vigilantes, then weapons just disappeared. It prompted the God Center to broadcast again, this time in the male voice.

"Greetings, my beloveds. We want to share some of the recent developments. We have spoken to every illegal gun owner on the planet and most importantly every gun owner too unstable for gun ownership. Those guns and all weapons we deemed unnecessary have been removed. Some people are turning their weapons into law enforcement, which we recommended. Those who did not cooperate gracefully or peacefully, and whose intentions were not good, we simply took their weapons away, like poof, gone. What was collected will be melted down and repurposed.

"Armies worldwide are weaponless. All the armed forces personnel are being retrained and reassigned to other jobs that will serve their communities. Everyone will be working for the common good globally.

"We know all about what you consider your 'rights'. It is not your right to take another life and that is what weapons are for, isn't it? You claim you need protection, that that is your right to protect yourself. From what, exactly? Think about it. And hunting? There was a day when if you didn't hunt, you didn't eat. Those days are over. So is the sport, we can't believe you made a sport of this killing in the first place.

"Oh my people learn to live in harmony. Respect all life, human and animal. If you need a gun to protect you from lions, bears or a crazed coyote attack, you can learn to communicate with animals just as you do with other humans, so they don't kill you. We will provide you with training, just ask. The Aborigines have been doing it for millennia, by the way. It's entirely possible to communicate with animals.

"It might help if you drop your thinking that they are lesser beings than you. The arrogance here needs to melt away. We understand it was written in that Bible book that God supposedly gave you 'dominion' over all animals on the planet. Hogwash. We created all life, and the idea of living in harmony has yet to be achieved here. You do not have dominion over animal life, please correct your thinking and be respectful toward life, human and animal.

"Yes, we know your Bible book said you have dominion over the Earth. That is definitely not something out of our mouth! It is more of your arrogance. We made all life, and we designed the Earth for you to care for and respect. We haven't seen any of this. We see you disrespecting animal life and certainly not giving the Earth much concern as you pollute it, rob it of its resources, and kill the soil with your chemicals. You have a responsibility living on this planet. It does not include 'rights' which you have certainly taken to an extreme level.

"Why are we doing this? Do you know what we have seen humans do over the past few thousand years? Your history is violent and loveless. It has been a never-ending series of wars and ethnic cleansing.

"We have seen all your stabbings, beheadings, massacres of an unbelievable scale, bombs, and burning people on stakes, it's all been endless. You are done destroying what we made. We made you. Did you not hear *Thou shalt not kill?* Do you think that only applies to mosquitoes? Or that only applies to whatever little nuisance you have? Do you think if this person is my 'enemy' it's okay to kill that human being – because he is what, a different color, a different nationality, and a different culture? Or are you just angry with them?

"It doesn't matter how on this Earth you try to justify taking another life. We want you to stop it. You couldn't follow a simple commandment of not killing so we are forced to take away from you the weapons you use. There will be no more killing of anything here. Yes, we are lecturing. Let us just say you need to hear all of this so you can change your thinking and behavior."

Lieutenant Bristol in Chicago was two years away from retirement. His wife, Phyllis, had been receiving treatment for breast cancer. As he listened to the God Center he was filled with hope. Hope that his wife's cancer would disappear, hope that the gangs that ravaged the city would not terrorize the citizens anymore, and hope that he would make it to his retirement without getting shot himself. He knew a lot about killings. It was his job. Violence, so much violence! He found himself choking up while listening to the God Center. At last, hope!

"Your weapons association is a very wealthy organization. They 'pride' themselves on making huge contributions to politicians to increase gun ownership and fight off any restrictions from ever being legislated. Every time there has been a mass shooting, there is public outrage that gun laws aren't stricter. All of that is over. The association's money will be funding something good for mankind. Isn't that nice of them? I suggested they really go out with a bang! (More God humor because yes, we can be quite funny at times – it's called joy). It is amazing how much money is available for your makeover, isn't it? And please, United States, oh my people, this is not just about you. You are witnessing the changes all over the Earth.

"We remind you again, these changes are for the common good, to spread harmony and peace and love throughout the Earth. There are many resources here that are in dire condition. You know you did this. Much was done in the name of progress but not a great deal of thinking ahead about the ramifications and consequences.

"Let's just take one little thing---plastic---a good idea gone off the rails. Some of its uses, say for respiratory therapy, are wonderful. The point is the tubing can be life-saving. It's the fact that it doesn't degrade, shouldn't be burned and it will take centuries for some plastics to break down. We know that normally inventors don't usually think of how the product will end up because the thrill of the creation of whatever it is takes over. There is a natural excitement when things are invented, like wow, all the uses for this! What it will save us from in terms of labor, so many considerations. Oh, let's not forget the one about how much money we are going to make with this new thing! That thought alone tends to excite the most, doesn't it?

"Do you realize how close the oceans and their precious contents were to absolute death before we came? We are serious. What an emergency! Oh my people! We feel like parents who must deal with their child using markers on the wall, or the child who painted the family cat. How lazy and disrespectful you have been. Please note our intended use of the past tense. You were lazy and disrespectful but of course now all that will change as everything is changing. You are all being told from your Source, the God Center, how to live in harmony.

"We are bringing you a technology far superior to plastic that will be easily degraded. We have installed equipment in all municipalities to dispose of the existing plastics rather than clog up the Earth with them. All we ask in the future is that you think about what you do before you do it. Think about the Earth. Think about your privilege to be here. Treat the Earth and each other with respect. We do see everything, you know The Earth itself is a living thing, Mother Earth, you've called it. Just how are you treating your mother? The Earth is not your doormat, any more than your actual mother is, so we are encouraging respect."

After three days, the government in Washington had received constant communication and directions from the God Center pod overhead, as well as the representatives on the ground. Finally, there was total cooperation from everyone, at least on the surface. Knowing the minds and hearts as only the God Center can, certain people were being watched very closely.

Another conversation with the president began.

"We see you made your list of assets. It's not complete you know."

"Yes, it is! I consulted my attorneys. It's all here," the president replied quickly.

"The golf course in Scotland is not on your list. Maybe you left it off because it is not currently making any money for you? No matter. You destroyed the coastline, and the people of Scotland are suing you because of it. Not only did we just have them win against you, but your course is gone, and the land has been restored to its natural beauty before you botched it up."

"How did you do that? I paid a lot of money for that land. Where's my money?"

"OMP! You really don't have much money, but you do have more money than brains, I guess. We had thought the irony of your money providing housing and better living conditions in the Native American communities would be beautiful. Then we looked at your finances, had a chuckle or two, and decided it was better irony that the NRA pays for that. Indirectly it was guns, after all, that enforced the near extinction of our people."

"Your people? They are your people? So, you're Cochise? You're Indians? OK, look, I've had it! Who are you and what the hell are you doing to my country?"

"Do you know what love is?"

"What the fuck kind of answer is that?"

"OMP, do you know how hard it can be to love you right now? What are we doing to your country? This is not your country in terms of ownership. Once again, we are the God Center, not aliens as you constantly refer to us. You obviously cannot accept that we are the God Center. Do you know the story of Peter Pan by any chance?"

"Yeah, sure, the green-tights guy," he replied smugly.

"Do you know the story?" queried the God Center. "Yeah, sure he had a gang and went around robbing people and shooting arrows at people. He was a fucking criminal and they hanged him in the woods," the president replied with his standard arrogance.

"Did you know he robbed the rich to feed the poor?" the God Center inquired.

"He's a criminal!" the president shouted.

"But what was his intention? It appears that as usual, you don't understand the point. I doubt it was to build a golf course to make money with. We have been so amused at your total lack of history, science and in fact the only area you excel in appears to be intimidation. That is not the way to run a country," the God Center patiently explained, still hoping for understanding and cooperation.

"I was elected to run this country as I see fit and that is just what I am trying to do. You need to go away and let me be in charge again," the president said loudly, his face red with anger.

"We are sorry to inform you of this tiny little point that seems to evade you. We are not leaving until everything on Earth has been remedied, the evil has been eliminated, and peace and prosperity are felt by all. We cannot keep going over and over this for your benefit when you fight us on everything we say and do. This is the God Center you are dealing with. We made you. Obviously, something in the creation of you went a bit nuts but hey, no worries. What we create we can also scrap, just like an artist would do if the painting wasn't turning out. We have tried painting over you, just as an artist may paint over mistakes. But you? You throw the paint back at your creator. So, you have left us no choice," and without fanfare, or certainly any press coverage, the president was removed.

The God Center made little progress with the president and his removal was not important since the rest of the government was functioning much better. The president could never have handled having no power whatsoever, not to mention the obsolescence of his position going forward. The streamlining of procedural habits created efficiency, which is important if government is going to serve the people. Perhaps these traditional procedures had been created to serve someone's ego. The entire process of government was highly inefficient which led to so many problems the God Center was addressing. Government was now learning how to be efficiently working for the people and it was a totally new experience for the legislators.

There were the two major parties both hellbent on being in charge and "winning". As the God Center reps worked with them, there was a blending into one cohesive party, the Party of the People. The God Center was pleased to call it POP. This would be the only pop available on the planet, the pop or soda contributing to ill health and obesity was eliminated.

Of course, there are always a few hold outs that refused to cooperate. Given that they were in conversations with the God Center directly and still they would not cooperate, they were eliminated. No longer would progress for the people depend on a few rebels with inflated egos.

Other governments worldwide were having the same experience. Corruption gone. Dictatorship gone. Resistance to governmental restructuring brought instant eliminations. With each country given a new streamlined government, part of the education for the new leadership was how to share knowledge with other governments. This was the unification process needed to have the entire planet sharing, cooperating and doing everything it could to promote harmony throughout the world. No secrets, no weapons, especially those of mass destruction, no irritating arrogance.

The people going into the grocery stores across the United States were in a panic trying to find the junk they were addicted to and willing to pay any price for it. The God Center was very busy trying to reassure the people that they would not starve.

The male and female voice from the God Center alternated. Day One was male, Day Two female, and now Day Three is male again. The God Center heard all the rumbling conversations about the male/female voices and how their conversations were so 'ordinary' sounding, and not 'godlike'" Critics everywhere, comedians everywhere, and rebels too, would be taken care of one way or the other. In more than a few instances, the God Center reminded the people of their disrespect.

The old saying that you cannot please everyone roared its ugly head in the direction of the ultimate creator. It was intolerable, but the God Center gently reminded people who they were complaining about or criticizing. Of course, all this was shocking to the people and some just needed more time to "adjust", but disrespect had to be eliminated.

Many had been taught in their religions that God was vengeful would exact severe punishments on people disobeying. This was more fiction created to control the religious populations. Besides, how dare anyone to describe the nature of God? Mankind had created God to suit their needs. It was time for truth, truth about everything.

"We hear you, Marsha, Ted, and everyone." The God Center began. "Yes, there are things missing. They will not be coming back. The store has plenty of food, real food. Pete, we saw you hoarding. No hoarding! You can only have what you need for the rest of this week. A few of the companies producing chemically laden products are being converted to producing wholesome food and they are doing this as we speak. Others will be manufacturing other products needed for daily living. None of it is junk food."

Carrie and Alan arrived in the parking lot of their nearest grocery super store. It was hard to find a parking spot, but they finally did. Alan grabbed a grocery cart and went inside the store.

"This is shocking! Look, the fruit and vegetables are everywhere," Alan dodged around the other shoppers to find the snack aisle. "OMG, it's full of fruit."

Carrie started putting apples in their cart.

"What the hell are you doing?" Alan shrieked.

"I'm getting food for us! Seeing as we are both in the obese category, we will eat good food now because we have no choice. There is no choice, Alan!"

"Well, I hate fruit!" he mumbled.

"Alan, we both wanted to lose weight. And from what we are hearing from the broadcasts, this is all being done so we can live healthy lives. I'm okay with this since we have no choice anyway," Carrie replied, while adding oranges to their basket.

Alan could not calm down.

"Carrie!" he screamed. "I can't eat this crap!"

"Alan, hush!" Carrie hissed. "Don't go makin' a scene here. Everyone will have to adjust to this, and that includes us."

Alan looked around at the other shoppers. Many comments about the whole "emptiness" of the store were heard, but for the most part, people took what was available and put it in their shopping baskets. Some were holding the fruits in their hands for the first time, looking at them as if they were totally foreign.

"We see you, Alan," the God Center said intervening. "We want all of you to enjoy good health and it begins with what you put in your mouth. This is how it is supposed to be. The super-sized grocery stores will be much smaller, and it will be easier to shop because everything in the store is good wholesome food so you cannot go wrong. No temptations for you to buy and eat things you know are not good for you. We are not taking all your 'pleasures' away, but we are telling you to spread out your indulgent tendencies to a treat now and then. Then it will be a treat.

"You human beings are electric energy. Your bodies are simply containers for that energy. When we see the outrageous conditions of your containers, or bodies, it is disrespectful. Honor what you have been given, a shell for containment of your God-infused energy. Love and respect yourselves, as the God Center does. Nutrition is needed to keep your bodies in optimum condition. Instead, you have fallen for all the junk that makes you obese and crushes the vital organs, impeding your health and progress.

"Between food and religion, we know this is a lot at one time. How else would you think we could affect all the changes this planet needs? Is this the right time for all of this? Yes! We had to intervene.

"We are aware of the didactic tone we are using. When you are trying to save humanity and the planet, there is a requirement for us to teach you and some of you are resistant to change. Yes, we are lecturing. How else do we remedy all that is needed, and teach you what your priorities need to be? Never forget, we are a part of you. You are a part of us. We have so much love for you that watching you disrespect yourselves to the degree that you are is absolutely intolerable. You are our children. Frankly, you need lectures!

"The God Center populates planets in galaxies you don't even know exist. In all our experiences, Earth is the worst. There is much hubris here. Humility needs to be spoon fed to Earth's inhabitants. And a heaping amount of racial tolerance. You are one people. ONE. None is above the other, nor is there such a thing as a 'favored' people. We do not have favorites, so whatever notions you have about your superiority needs to go.

"There are many health experts here, yet you chose not to listen to their dietary guidance. A few have, but we are talking about the majority. And, by the way, this is not the case globally. It's basically the United States. From our vantage point, assessing the Earth, you in the United States have the distinction of being the worst nutritionally speaking.

"The supposedly richest country on the planet where some spend hundreds on chemical foods, while some countries produce only two crops to survive on and they do survive. The contrast is devastating to us.

"We know that some of you think of this as boot camp. Call it whatever you want to, keeping in mind, this is not a game. This is survival for all humanity on this planet. The option to be removed is available to all. So far only 12,214 people have asked to be removed. We are sad that they didn't want to see the Earth at peace and thriving. It will be, very soon. As for the uncooperative group that has been removed, their numbers are not important. Trust us that these people would not have contributed to the common good.

"You might be interested in the fact that two of the bottled-water companies will continue to provide bottled water for emergency use only, and on a limited scale. It will no longer be sold in stores. You can quit crying about this. We found tons of plastic water bottles in the oceans, literally tons. You have shown yourselves to be too lazy and unconcerned about your garbage, despite warnings, repeated warnings, that you were polluting the oceans. You did not heed the warnings of how the chemicals in the plastic, when heated (think of it sitting in your hot car) cause hormonal disruptions. Enough already! You want to carry water with you throughout your day? Buy a thermos, a good one, so you won't toss it carelessly.

"Did you know France banned plastic water bottles? We didn't hear the French crying about it. They adjusted and so will you. Obviously, it is sad to us that many things going on in the European countries for the betterment of mankind did not make their way across the ocean. The United States hears about it, or reads about it, then says oh that's nice! Some wonder why those progressive things aren't going on in the United States. We wondered too. And now it's all getting fixed.

"Sorry, we digress. The bottled water companies not producing bottled water have the assignment to fix the water in Flint, Michigan which is being tended to as we speak. How this happened and yet was never addressed, is beyond terrible. We really do have to do everything for you, don't we? That's how bad things are here. We know it's not as much the fault of the people but rather a very constipated government that should take better care of its people.

"Many towns have inadequate water – we know about it and we are tending to every one of them. Maybe if all the people protested about the water instead of all the other things you protest about, maybe, just maybe the government may have risen to the occasion. Hmm, doubtful.

"Priorities you should have had are now being ordered, issues addressed, problems rectified. You will be given a clean healthy planet and the opportunity to keep it that way. The same thing with your health. Love yourselves and love the God Center enough to thrive."

Alan and Carrie left the grocery store with two bags of fruit, vegetables, rice, pasta and canned goods. Carrie tried to cajole Alan by telling him about all the new recipes she would be trying. "You'll see, Alan. We'll get thin on this program and maybe cure some of our ailments in the process. Let's be optimistic."

Alan was still grumbling.

"Look Alan, do you want to be removed? Do you want to leave me?"

"Absolutely not," he said, kissing her cheek. "I'm sorry. I'm just having a real hard time accepting what is going on."

"I know, Alan. Me, too. But let's try to enjoy this. It really is an opportunity to renovate ourselves!"

Logan woke up early but had nowhere but the kitchen to go to where hopefully the coffee was waiting. He smiled to himself as the sun was streaming through the bedroom windows and sighed. Last night was good. He was so glad that Jessie handled her information so well that Patti was intrigued. He made a mental note to check in with Manuel to see how things were going in his family.

Jessie showed the pictures she had taken herself and also pictures in books of the celestial events painted everywhere across the globe in caves, on walls, in and around ancient temples. The pictures showed angels or gods coming from the sky, some going as far back as 12,000 years ago.

"Why didn't the archaeologists take this seriously? The art is primitive, but they wrote their history that way didn't they?" Patti asked Jessie.

"Many of the ancient culture had writing, some of which may be in the Vatican, but most of the texts were destroyed in the name of war, especially during the crusades. In most of the cases, it wasn't war as much as it was the Spanish Conquistadors in the 15th[th] and 16th[th] centuries who destroyed the most. They were serving the church who demanded complete compliance with church rules.

"The Mayan civilization was so advanced! They knew astronomy, mathematics, physics and engineering on a scale that was unbelievable to the Spanish. It probably terrified them. While the Maya did have outlandish sacrifices of human life to honor their 'gods', their culture was leap years ahead of the Spaniards, who thought since there was no way to convert these people to Catholicism, they'd best be destroyed. The church was the only source of information allowed. Keeping the people ignorant was a great benefit to the church. Much easier to control, ya know," Jessie said.

"Yes, I always found it strange that knowledge was not revered, especially in the church circles. I mean look at the story of Adam and

Eve. She took the apple from the tree of knowledge, like this was a bad thing? And then there's the church for centuries and centuries, condemning people and cultures for their advanced knowledge. Like if it didn't originate with church, it should not exist," Patti replied.

"You know about Galileo?" Jessie asked Patti.

"Yes, Logan told me the other day. I had no idea. The fact that the church could dispose of anyone that didn't swallow their stories, I mean, I'm shocked. How many cultures have you studied, Jessie?" she asked.

"All of them. I've been at this for over twenty years, and I've traveled to see ruins all over the world. It's been an exciting education but then there's the frustrating part. Archaeologists and scientists saw what I saw but for whatever reason they would not commit their reputations to just come out and say it. We were actively learning from 'others' for thousands of years, worldwide, like I mean everywhere," Jessie answered.

"But why? Why won't they come out and say it? We've been visited and taught physics and engineering that advanced mankind," Patti asked.

Logan stepped in with "Patti, the church literally tried to run the world. All this 'infallibility' stuff, as if only they could tell people what they wanted them to hear! Galileo was a heretic because he dared to go with the science. He was right, they were wrong, and it took thousands of years for them to admit it? So today, if it comes out that some scientist shows the world how he put the pieces together and declared not only did we have visitors from the Pleiades, but we may have come from there --- what does the church do with their infallible stories then?"

"I get it, Logan. Is this why you would never go to church with me?" Patti inquired with a teasing smile.

"In a nutshell, yes" Logan admitted.

Jessie continued, "Now Hawaii is so interesting. The people there actually believe they were from another place and were sent to Earth.

Isn't it funny that out of all the cultures on Earth currently, they are the only living people acknowledging their roots?

"Plus, they have been a hot spot of 'visitations'. When you think about it, it is remote on the planet, and it would be a great place for a portal. I'll tell you about portals later, but there is a spot on the big island, believed to be where the ancient aliens came. There are Hawaiians who hold celebrations there and they are waiting for the return of their 'ancestors'. It was their belief that they would be the only people on the planet that would greet 'aliens' with aloha rather than a gun."

"Really?" Logan said. "They might be right. The Pentagon scrambled when the orbs were visible and I'm sure if the God Center had not disabled them, however they did that, shots would have been fired. It seems to be our nature to attack whatever is unknown with a shoot first, ask questions later approach."

"Of course, they would have tried to shoot them down," Jessie said. "The God Center has it right when they say there is a lot of arrogance here. We would shoot first and ask questions later, you're so right Logan."

"I'm sure glad they didn't, or couldn't shoot," added Patti. "We would be headed for one hell of an ending with all the problems on this planet. I'm just amazed at all you've shared, Jessie. Can you recommend some books for me to read? I'm really interested in the ancient cultures now. It appears some knowledge has been lost, pieces scattered or hidden from us."

Remembering last evening's discussions with Patti and Jessie, Logan went downstairs to the kitchen for his morning coffee. Patti was there on her laptop, "Good morning hon, what are you up to?" he asked kissing the top of her head as he walked by her on his way to the coffeemaker.

"I'm doing research. Jessie is so knowledgeable and I'm checking out some of the sites she talked about last night. I think this is all so incredible. Aren't you fascinated?" she inquired.

"Not as much as you are. I am familiar with much of this. Besides, I've heard a lot about Jessie's frustration that evidence was being ignored just to preserve and protect the church and its stories. It will all be tumbling down now. Can't wait to hear about what is found in the top-secret archives of the Vatican now!" Logan said.

"So, what are you going to do today?" Patti asked.

"Beyond calling Manuel, I may take Buster out for a good romp in the park. He's not used to me being home. Have you noticed how he is following me around very closely? Kinda cute. I think he misses me when I go to work. You need me to do anything for you around the house?"

"I'm sure I'll think of something," she said laughing. "I'm not used to you being home either. I'll have to work on making that honey do list for you, but right now I'm happy just doing research. Who knows? I may write a book someday on all the signs we missed, or purposely missed as the case may be," Patti said.

"Honey, that's a great idea. I think that book should be written. But I have to tell you, the books out there right now regarding ancient aliens and the technologies of God are out there already. If you want, we could go over to the library this afternoon. I'd like to get a few books myself," Logan commented, happy that his wife was no longer a mess over her religion being a sham.

He came up behind Patti who was sitting on a bar stool at their kitchen island. He wrapped his arms around her, kissing the back of her neck playfully.

She started giggling, "Logan, do I sense romance or are you just playing around?"

"I think you need a nap, sweetheart." That had been their "code" when the boys were around the house. Patti slid off her bar stool to face Logan. They embraced with a hungry passion. Pushing back so she could see his face, "Yes, I so do need a nap. Let's go mess up a bed!" and the two, holding hands went upstairs.

Later that day, Logan called Manuel.

"Hey buddy, I've got a box in my car for you with your personal items from the office. How's everything going?" Logan inquired.

"Hi, Logan. Thanks for calling. It's been a weird vigil. Silvia's entire family has camped out here, lighting candles and praying. At least they've stopped their wailing, but man, I'd love to go to work just to get out of here," he replied.

"I can drive over with your box and take you out for a coffee, or drink, whichever you need most," Logan offered.

"Great! How soon can you get here?" Manuel asked.

"I'll leave right away and spring you out of there in less than an hour. Anything else you need?" Logan said.

"No, I'm good. Just get here," Manuel smiled to himself as he hung up the phone.

"Sylvia, Logan's bringing me some stuff from the office and we're going out for a coffee. Do you need anything from the store while I'm out?" Manuel asked, hoping for a quiet exit.

Sylvia and her family came from Mexico. They were a tight knit family and strict Catholics. Manuel was born in the United States, but his family emigrated from Nicaragua. Sylvia was the youngest of six children, all born in Mexico coming to the States fifteen years ago. Family gatherings were a minimum of 32 people, all of whom were crowded into Manuel's home. Only a few of them were fluent in English.

"Oh Manuel, you don't have a job now? What are we going to do?" she said tearfully.

"Come on Sylvia don't cry about this. Everything will work out just fine. I think it's time for your family to go back to their homes. This is not an invasion; we are safe and they can watch the broadcasts at their own homes."

Sylvia's mother overheard the exchange and took the opportunity to announce to the family that she would be leaving to go home.

"Oh mama, you can stay here if you don't want to go home by yourself." Sylvia said, feeling a bit ashamed of her husband's loud hint that everyone leave.

"Pita and Geraldo will be with me, Sylvia. Do not worry," she replied in Spanish, as she started to gather up her belongings.

The family was exiting as Logan pulled up to Manuel's house. He waved to a carload of them departing as he parked across the street. There were still several cars in the driveway. He got out of his car, grabbed the box from his trunk and walked up to the front door just as it was opening.

"Oh, you scared me!" Mama said, startled to see Logan.

"I'm sorry, ma'am. I've come to bring Manuel this box," Logan apologized.

The chaos with the family all leaving, hugging, and saying long goodbyes made Logan roll his eyes when he saw Manuel in the midst. Manuel nodded in his silent agreement. Manuel pointed to the kitchen where he wanted Logan to leave his box getting him out of the crowded living room.

Once in the quieter kitchen, Manuel came in shaking his head. "Oh brother, what a production. Be very glad you don't have a family like this," he said.

"I guess this has been quite the shock for them, huh?" Logan asked.

"You wouldn't believe it. I thought I'd go nuts with all the crying. To say this family is full of fanatically religious people would be an understatement. I'm so glad they've calmed down, but better than that, I'm glad they are leaving," Manuel said. "Let's get out of here!"

They took the back door out of the kitchen, Manuel yelling goodbye and saying he'd be back later.

As Logan drove, Manuel said "I'm hungry. Let's just stop at Appleby's. That OK with you?"

"Sure, whatever you want. I just wanted to spring you from that chaos," Logan said. He admired Manuel. Overcoming his poor background, getting his doctorate and then some, Manuel was the poster child for perseverance.

"Hey man, I really appreciate this. Sylvia will be okay when her family leaves. Seems there is a real bent for drama in that group. Like whoever does the most wailing wins or something. I just cannot relate to any of that. I went outside a few times for a smoke to calm down. I didn't want to scream at her family but honestly, how I managed not to is a miracle in itself."

Manuel has the highest level of education in his family, having a PhD in astronomy. His specialty is astrogeology, examining rocks, terrain and material in space. Besides his fluidity in Spanish, he also has a working fluency in German and Russian. Knowing Sylvia and her family had only the basics of education made it difficult for Manuel. He made sure to be humble and polite when he was around the family. They thought he was a good man, but instead of calling him intelligent, they regarded him as eccentric, the family oddball. It was easier for them to accept him as odd, rather than intellectually superior.

"Hey Manuel, you wouldn't happen to have any of your 'smokes' with you, would you?" Logan asked, thinking it sure would be a good time to mellow out.

"Not on me, but I know where the dispensary is and if they have any buds left, we're golden. Go down to Oriel Avenue. It's on the corner," Manuel said.

You may say I'm a dreamer but I'm not the only one.
I hope someday you will join me and the world will be as
ONE.

John Lennon

Zytaria

The God Center spoke to researchers, physicists, nuclear scientists, astrophysicists and all who participated in scientific research on planet Earth. Fermi National Accelerator Laboratory in Illinois had detected the shadow of a supermassive black hole at the center of the Messier 87 galaxy. While the discoveries made there seemed progressive, the God Center brought much more advanced knowledge to the 4,000 researchers there from 50 countries. The information the God Center shared was jaw-dropping. The God Center then sent a representative there to coordinate changes they needed to "update" their laboratories.

CERN, in Switzerland, contains 12,000 scientists from 70 countries working at the European Organization for Nuclear Research. Also, NRCKI, CAS, INFI, in Russia, China and Italy respectively. Unknown to most of the population, the most sharing done on Earth were research partnerships sharing globally, some of them anyway. The God Center sent representatives to all the locations globally in order to coordinate research projects on the new intelligence the scientists were receiving.

There were enlightened conversations on the origin of high-energy cosmic rays, quarks and many topics. The God Center delighted in the questions and provided all research centers with information that would encourage and advance each center. A few solutions were given in certain areas that the God Center wanted to boost for the advancement of humanity.

Overall, the global sharing was a theme to spread beyond just the scientific community. The God Center knew Earth is thousands of years behind the other colonies they established. If only they could see the other planets and how they run themselves! The God Center offered hope, offered another chance, and offered unlimited love.

It appeared on Earth, most people were not interested in research, science or things going on outside of their own personal little worlds. Such a contrast to the other planets! There were amusements for the people elsewhere, but not to the extent they were on Earth.

The God Center populated many planets throughout the universe. There were several that the God Center created about the same time as the planet Earth. As time went on, several were destroyed; the "experiment" went horribly wrong with the multi-racial approach. While things were grim on Earth, the God Center did not want to destroy another of its creations. The God Center wanted Earth to be one of those progressive, peaceful planets. The intervention on Earth was the God Center's special project. Comparisons with the other planets made Earth appear hopeless. Had things gone too far?

On Zytaria for instance, the early messengers sent to all the new "developments" led to their progress. They had space travel and the planet itself is what some would call utopia. Similar to Earth in many ways, yet the differences are startling.

Zytaria has seven continents separated by vast oceans: the topography and climates much the same as Earth. Each continent was populated with different races of people, again similar to Earth. There are portals on each continent of Zytaria for communication and travel that were shown to the inhabitants in the ancient times by 'visitors' of even more advanced cultures. They evolved technically and scientifically since they had been given that knowledge and used it.

When given the advanced knowledge in science, physics and mathematics the people of Zytaria became very progressive. There was no destruction of knowledge, rather it was treasured and expanded upon, quite the opposite of Earth.

When they were able to discover the other continents on the planet, it was done with complete respect. Yes the people on each continent looked different and had differences in culture, foods and traditions, but all were happy to share and learn from one another. Likewise, with their advancement on Zytaria, once space travel began there were visits to other neighboring planets, again peacefully and with sharing in mind. The travelers from Zytaria encountered human 'like' peoples, but never was there fear or judgment, even though appearances varied greatly. They live in a peaceful and respectful galaxy, eager to learn about others, sharing technologies. There is an exchange where people can visit or even temporarily reside as guests on other planets.

On Zytaria agriculture is revered and cooperatives were developed to trade crops between the continents. Farms are located outside of each city, supplying the people with fresh meats and vegetables. There are Nutrition Centers, the equivalent of grocery stores on Earth but not as large as the supersized stores on Earth. Foods are easily imported and exported between the continents due to the speed of their transportation systems.

The educational system on Zytaria is vastly different. Children begin school at age 4 where they learn languages of the other continents throughout their schooling. Before the age of four, children spend their days at the Nurturing Center, receiving early education there.

As a part of a child's education, they are given every opportunity to experience all sports, and music, lessons available for any instrument they wished to try as well as lessons for sports. The encouragement to try anything and everything is ingrained in every area of life. Every child has an assignment to spend weeks on a local farm, learning how food is grown, and how animals are raised. It is a requirement.

Every child looks forward to being 6 when they spend time with their parents at work, learning about whatever business or profession their parents had chosen.

By the age of 10, a child is allowed to choose whatever subjects they enjoy the most. They are still required to take basic reading and math regardless of their chosen area of study. Their education is tailored to whatever area the child instinctively is interested in. This is not a permanent "major" however as the child could always change it to explore in depth another subject. Amazingly changes tend to be unusual. In fact, adults are free to change their careers without punitive consequences. The result is people happy to work at what they love also realizing their contribution to the common good of all. Every job is considered honorable as well as an honor.

School is full time with one day off per week and a vacation for summer and winter solstice each for three weeks. The emphasis on education is evident in the advanced society. Given the freedom to excel in the area of their choice, children truly enjoy their schooling.

Advanced education is available for all, the length of which is determined by the field of study. For some, formal education may be complete by 16; others may study well into their 20's. Everyone has a job to do to contribute to the common good of all.

It is rare that a young person would not know what job they would have since they were allowed to choose for themselves what area of study they preferred. Factories needed workers, drivers were needed for mass transportation and delivering products. These positions are so important to the functioning of society that it is not considered a "lower" position. Salaries for all work are equalized so there is not the push to make more, have more as in other planets like Earth. Not being enticed by higher salaries, along with the absence of greed, proved very stabilizing on Zyhtaria.

Families are not controlled in terms of having children, or how many to have. Mothers are given the child's first year off to stay at home if they so choose, but rarely do they take that long. Workdays and school hours were compatible, being 8 a.m. to 2 p.m. giving people time to pursue their interests, work in the community garden, engage in sports, as well as it could be time for home maintenance. Everything was accomplished as a family unit, meaning everyone helped with maintenance. It was the responsibility of each individual to live in harmony, by all contributing. This was not elective.

There is a great reverence for maintaining a stable environment. The indoor cleanliness of their homes is carried to the out of doors. Zytaria has beautiful gardens and parks, kept pristine by those dedicated to the botanical sciences. Neighborhoods have community garden space where they can grow fruits and vegetables and all the parks are surrounded by fruiting trees.

Housing is not extravagant, but there are differences in the architecture, layouts and color that make them individualized. There are set prices for homes, which are a bit more expensive than communal building living.

The arts, music and theater have a presence appreciated by all, without craziness. If you were sharing your talent in these areas, it was considered your job and for that, those attending concerts or theater applauded on a job well done without any idolization. Salaries were set, raises given, but nowhere on Zytaria are there millionaires. The thought of anyone having too much money, and thereby trying to control and manipulate due to the power associated with wealth, is considered criminal. The currency on the planet evolved into one currency throughout the continents, making trade and travel seamless. Bartering is used more than money, sharing being the universal standard that is adhered to.

SAVED

There are no guns and crimes are rare. If indeed a crime is committed, the offender is sent to the Attrition Center for counseling. It is not a prison but a place to honor justice and truth and identify problems. Sometimes all that is needed is a new job, a chance to try something new, so more training is given. The counselor is available for daily sessions until the problem is solved. It would be a rare occasion for anyone doing physical harm to another. Love and respect were taught from the cradle. Other lessons in nonjudgmental attitudes are taught early on.

There are Protection People (police) in every municipality. They enforce orderly conduct in the event there is a disturbance of the peace and harmony. They are well trained in the physical and martial arts but carry no weapons.

All medical services are free. Each person pays a tithe to the medical association yearly. Because of their food supply and herbs readily available, illness of any kind is very rare. There is the Rejuvenation Center for surgery, if necessary, and to fix broken bones. In lieu of vaccines, everyone receives a wellness shot annually. It boosts the immunity system, as a preventative. Between organically raised foods and animals, health threats from chemicals and pesticides are unknown.

If the citizens of Zytaria have anything close to idolization, it would be to science, astronomy, and physics.

Citizens on all the continents are given all the education needed for whatever field of study they want to explore. It is not uncommon for people to switch jobs to enter a new field. Education is revered.

Everyone on the planet of Zytaria has what they need; food, housing, and a job that contributes to the good of all. The president of any company makes only slightly more than his/her employees.

Their government is simply run by delegates from all areas on the planet coming together for a globally run operation. Citizens participate with their local delegates in meetings each month to address issues. The delegates then meet in preparation for the Continental Exchange, which

109

is also held once a month. Delegates from all the continents assemble with their presentations. Whatever issues need action, it is immediate, no red tape, no committees or bureaucracy. Elections for the delegates are held every 10 solstices, or every five years.

To fund the government, Benefit Fees are paid by the citizens each solstice and the amount is predicated on salaries. This allows for all medical and educational services to be "free". The people are allowed to "retire" from a paid position providing they still contribute by participating in something. The elderly are usually found volunteering in the Nurturing Center, helping children learn languages, caring for gardens or libraries, but they can contribute to society in whatever way they choose. The time spent doing this "work" is entirely up to the individual. The main objective is to remain active and share your gifts and talents regardless of age. It helps give the elderly a sense of purpose and inclusion. Because of their healthy lifestyles, the health of seniors on Zyhtaria is excellent.

There are competitions in sports, like Earths Olympics for added entertainment on an annual basis. Many athletes "retire" as coaches. Regionally there are sports competitions weekly, the final winners of each make it to the annual event. Sport centers are always open to the public for nominal fees.

Transportation throughout each city is by monorail. Employers pay for their employee's annual pass. Going from one continent to another is on air boats that travel at the speed of sound, 760 miles per hour. Fossil fuels are a thing of the distant past, having advanced technologies on the planet. Solar, wind and water provided power. The use of crystals is common for their more advanced technologies. The solar devices used aren't the turbines used on Earth. Some are in the shapes of trees, located everywhere, with each leaf producing power as they wave in the breeze. Some solar devices look like flowers in small windmill-like shapes.

Meditation is taught as soon as school starts at age 4. Meditation centers are located in every neighborhood and each home has a meditation room. People gather for talks and meditating in the centers on Rest Day. This would be the closest thing to "going to church" Zytarians experience. The use of crystal singing bowls is popular. In summer, there are drumming ceremonies in the parks, and they are well attended.

Being physically fit, as well as spiritually fit is an unwritten law on Zytaria. Walking, running and playing sports are enjoyed by all no matter what age.

Zytaria has storms, Zquakes (earthquakes) and volcanoes. Whenever a natural disaster occurs anywhere on the planet, rescue, rebuilding or whatever help an area needs galvanizes a complete response and immediately. People stand ready to assist in any way they can because they know it is their responsibility to care for their planet. Even a Zquake on another continent would be responded to by all the continents coming together to assist with whatever would be needed.

Holidays revolve around the two solstices, Winter Solstice and Summer Solstice. It is a time of concerts, sports competitions, banquets and parties. Traveling to other continents, one can experience the same celebrations in other cultures, and this was encouraged. People on Zytaria live healthy, productive lives averaging 120 years, but their technology is working on extending that lifetime.

Everyone has access to the news broadcasts on the communication screens located in each home. The emphasis on progress in all sciences and what is going on in each of the continents is the basic daily report. The news is always positive and ends with a list of ways to help other people, cities or continents. Sharing and helping others is taught and practiced throughout Zytaria.

The God Center knew that Earth had all the potential to be as progressive as Zytaria, but things had gone terribly wrong almost from the very beginning. Suppression of knowledge is a huge reason. Hiding the truth of the people's origin didn't help. The fact that there was a story in the Bible book about being forbidden to eat from the Tree of Knowledge certainly did damage. It was so ingrained in people believing that, that it hindered much of the early progress on Earth.

Could bringing some of Zytaria to Earth make a difference?

Acknowledging the good that is already in your life is
the foundation for abundance.

Eckhart Tolle

DAY FOUR

"Welcome to day four! Lots of surprises for you," the female God Center voice said.

"We are showing you continuous streaming from everywhere on all forms of media. We understand there are many who still do not believe what we say we are. If you needed 'proof' to believe the God Center, you certainly have it. Who else could do what we are doing?

"How enlightened you will all be after this! There is no human being on this planet that cannot hear us; we went so far as to cure the deaf among you so literally everyone can hear the God Center. Our visit to your planet is truly a first for us. We have blown up several of our projects that have gone too far in the wrong directions. What made the difference with Earth? Aren't you curious?

"Spiritual communities and good people, some of which you even made fun of for hugging trees. There was a brief time when 'hippies' were rejecting the corporate world and what it stood for, the greed, the pretenses, the business philosophies focused on cut-throat practices.

"Believe it or not, they had the right idea back then, wanting to just live off grid in peace and love. They were the first truly planet-respectful people we witnessed in America. What do you know of the Basque nation? Look into it. They have the lowest crime rate in that part of the Earth, again good people.

"That's what saved Earth – good people -- as well as our crazy love for humanity. We heard your cries for fairness, justice and having a chance at a good life. We saw what was going on and how the class divides increased truly out of proportions. Greed and the quest for power over others led you to this mess we are fixing.

"We saw the wars, always wars. Just because the United States was involved in conflicts, but never on American soil (well, since your Civil War anyway!) there are many wars going on, too many! Perhaps you don't know about it because there is a general lack of global awareness here. This should not be! The over-all global knowledge is slim, and the interest level seems to be based on money, weapons and fame. We do laugh at your so-called pro-life people who don't educate themselves about life in other places being in danger.

"Burkina Faso is having ethnic clashes, the Central African Republic fights between Moslems and Christians, the Democratic Republic of the Congo has wars against its rebel groups, and Egypt has war against Islamic militants of the Islamic State branch, a civil war in Libya, Mali, Mozambique, Somalia, and more. You may personally not be aware of this, or in fact, even know where these countries are located. It's all a proliferation of madness to us. But this is all happening on your planet. Let's see if we can't learn about the rest of your world, like expand your love to your neighbors."

Patti and Logan were having breakfast on their patio overlooking the garden. "Did you know about these conflicts in other countries?" Patti asked Logan.

"The Pentagon rarely shared that information with our department, unless it was something our forces might become involved in. It is strange though, now that the God Center brings this up. Again, we the people are left out. I'm so glad all of this is coming out, aren't you?"

"Well sure. We should know what is happening on this planet. However, I think the United States always assumes the role of being the world's police, usually without asking if people elsewhere even want our help."

"No shit! Other than kicking ass on the Nazi's for their extermination project, we should stay out of other countries. It's not like we have the most perfect country here. I mean look at all the God Center is doing. We could have, and should have done something about hunger, homelessness and all the messes here. And where do we put our money? 725 billion to the Pentagon, mostly for our military but who knows what else they do with the money?" Logan said angrily.

"Logan don't work yourself up now. All the wrongs here are being made right, at last. Jessie is coming over today to show me a book she put together with all her pictures from her travels. Since she's not working right now, she's keeping herself busy with her book. Hope you can stay around and join us, Patti offered.

Logan gave her a thumbs up as the God Center continued.

"We have intervened everywhere. No sense in partially addressing what's wrong – this is a big planet. We want for you all to have more global awareness. If there is one rotten apple in the barrel, it can spoil the barrel – get it? We know who the rotten apples are. They are being given a choice to change or be removed.

"That brings up another topic, related to global activity, foreign aid. Here is a brief list of the top ten countries receiving aid from the United States.

Israel 3.3 billion
Jordan 1.52 billion
Egypt 1.43 billion
Tanzania 547 million
Kenya 544 million
Uganda 533 million

Mozambique 522 million

South Africa 482 million

Zambia 467 million

Iraq 454 million

"There are more, but wow, isn't that something? How generous on the surface of it all. You realize of course, the people in those countries don't benefit from the money given to them. They are hungry, they need medical attention, and they need sustainable living conditions.

"We are working with everyone on the planet. The United States will no longer send money to these countries. It is the funding of these countries that has encouraged corruption in governments. The United States government can now spend that money on free health care and helping pharmaceutical companies begin production of herbal pills and tinctures and using only the few drugs that work.

"The cancer industry and its toxic treatments are gone. There are so many cancer 'cures' that have been swept under the proverbial rug because of greed. The cures are non-toxic and will be available to all.

"All the beautiful cancer centers are being converted to natural treatment centers. You won't need them very long. Once the toxins you've been eating and breathing disappear, so will cancer. You can use the treatment center buildings for apartments later since there are far too many of them, and housing is needed for many.

"Nurses and doctors are being retrained away from the toxins being used to the God intended natural ways. Natural remedies have been scoffed at as 'alternative medicine.' It is original, not alternative. Drugs are the alternative. Some work, most do not."

"Monies from this windfall are also being appropriated for mass transportation, which is desperately needed to service people conveniently, thereby reducing some of your infamous traffic. We are fixing America with the money that should have been spent in America for Americans.

"Each country is being helped to be functional and self-sustaining for its people. It is no longer the American taxpayers funding a myriad of areas that do not benefit America. Not to mention the fact that most of the money you've dished out to foreign governments never went to the intended targets."

"Brian, did you see that? Look at the rain!" Mike exclaimed.

"I know! Wow. This must be God – although I can't believe I'm even saying this!"

"Yeah, it's kinda hard to be an atheist now, isn't it?"

"Shit, you've got that right!" They were watching the God Center's global streaming of the different parts of the Earth that were changing on Brian's laptop.

Mike's eyes were tearing up. "I know you'll think I'm crazy, Brian, but I've dreamed of this day, of being 'rescued' from the illness, from the deceit, the money-centered lives we seem to live," his tears making him choke the last words out.

Mike and Brian married last year, amid the protests of gay marriages. Mike worked as a reservationist at United Airlines, and Brian was a mechanic for the same company. Brian had received what Mike thought was a death sentence, cancer of the colon. He was at home recuperating from the surgery that diagnosed that condition.

"I think the miracles we are seeing now will pale in comparison to what the world will be like when the God Center is finished, he said, putting his arm around his tearful partner.

"Brian, the God Center said there are cures for cancer so you're going to be just fine, we all will be, I'm sure!" Mike said.

"The homeless tents are gone!" Gary observed driving to downtown Portland. "Just last week this whole underpass was packed with tents and garbage."

"Amazing. I can't believe what I'm seeing," his wife Terri said.

"I wonder if they are gone from downtown too."

"I bet they will be gone. This is God doing all this and we should trust that he wants everything nice here – I mean healthy and peaceful, not just pretty. I'm touched, aren't you?" she replied while wiping a tear. "I always felt so badly for those people. Life has been hard for them and yeah I know everyone was repulsed that there were tents everywhere, but can you imagine? Living in a tent?"

"No, I sure can't imagine. Thank God something is being done to help them," Gary said. "I've been such a pessimist, saying the world is going to hell. Now I feel full of hope."

It was a tremendous boost to the God Center's presence to be showing the global changes for everyone's viewing. Many, who were still doubtful of the future, were experiencing miracles on their screens everywhere. Hope was in the air.

"The God Center came to right the wrongs, fix the broken, feed the hungry and to teach. We want to give you a quick repeat of a lesson that was given to you in a book by Brian Weiss, MD. Some words on love – you need to hear this. Quote *'Reach out with love and compassion to help others without concern for what you may gain. Whether you reach out to a few or to many is not important. The numbers do not matter; the act of reaching out with caring does.'* unquote.

"How many spiritual guidebooks have we sent to you via messengers? Hundreds. Dr. Weiss even entitled his book *'Messages from the Masters'*. So many writers have published words that were direct downloads from the God Center. We encourage you to read and expand yourselves spiritually. There is nothing wrong gathering together, as you may have done in the churches, to celebrate your spirits and commune with one another, In fact, good for you doing it. Just lose all the labels. Labels divide, they do not unite. Rather amusing you call yourselves the United States. We have seen none of that united stuff!

"There is always joy and love to share and that is a great opportunity. It may not be the same as your previous church services, but it really could be, just without the dogma. Use the gatherings to reach out to whoever in your congregation needs help. If you just go to go, to get what you can from the message, you are being selfish. Look around you. Talk to each other and share your needs. Make a community of love. Feel it. Speak it. Show it."

People all over the globe were watching TV's, laptops and screens everywhere in awe and astonishment. They could see for themselves the vast changes to landscapes, farm fields and cities now devoid of the tents and garbage. They saw reservoirs filling up faster than any normal gentle rain could do. Lake Mead in Nevada had not been at capacity since the summer of 1983. Until now. The Colorado River Basin, Lake Powell and the entire region received what it needed to be fully restored. Seeing this, the people of that area were instantly believers of the God Center and its mission to save the planet.

"The God Center would like to point out that the worlds' nuclear plants are gone. There is no button to press that will annihilate humans. The millions and billions used to build and maintain, are now eliminated, as well as the dangers. We have given you a safe method for unlimited power at no cost to you. The disaster in Japan was a warning. So was Chernobyl. Yet you do nothing? Your plants were so close to a total breakdown, several in particular. You would have annihilated yourselves. We feel the alternative sources we have given you will allow you to make progress in other areas of technology. We have shared much with your scientists, physicists and astro-engineers. It will help you to make up for the progress you desire in many areas of your lives."

Countries experiencing the ravages of conflicts, starvation and abuse were viewed with elation, all issues having been "addressed". The planet was getting closer to being in good order. The God Center would touch it all eventually and now all the people near screens could witness the miraculous improvements. As the viewing of the changes continued, more hearts were being changed as well.

"You can see for yourselves now just what the God Center has been telling you it would do. We are hearing many of you in shock. The God Center has no limits. Change is coming – everywhere!

"Some of you are upset. We understand. You need to see the big picture, which is another way of saying don't take everything personally. Our work with the NFL and AFL for instance, take your time to see the overall benefits rather than feeling personal deprivation. We aren't eliminating sports; you'll still have your football and other games. We're changing the financial dynamics.

"We capped salaries to the highest being $100,000. All medical is free now, so no worries about saving money for those post-sport injuries and issues. Those with huge million-dollar contracts should be proud of their contribution to education. It may take them personally a while to get to that point, but nonetheless, people can now afford to see the games in person. Ticket prices are slashed, parking is free, and it will be affordable entertainment. Just the fact that your Super Bowl has seats for thousands of dollars is unbelievable. The education system needs trump entertainment.

"This was another priority you had all wrong! All new textbooks are being printed, God Center supervised of course, to tell the truth and nothing but the truth, so help me ME. Many schools are going through renovation as we speak. Some inner-city schools and rural areas were deplorable and unsafe.

"There is now funding for schools to have healthy lunches, teacher raises, and reinforced music, art and home-skills classes. If you don't introduce children to art and music, society is only breeding, not educating children. Re-prioritizing everything for you has been a major project with us. Again, the United States was pretty 'off" shall we say? And no, Kevin, we did not ask your permission! We hear you screaming. The mere fact that you honestly think we need to ask your permission? Seriously!"

It was a time of great enlightenment for Earth. While mankind was all about the quest for the secret forces of the universe, here, right here, was the God Center. Many scientists were having discussions with the God Center. Questions were answered for them by the absolute Source. Their newfound knowledge would benefit all enormously. The scientists and researchers had many questions and they received answers on everything: cures for diseases, answers about the universe, and ways to make technology safe and efficient were given by the God Center. So many answers in fact that a few scientists were beginning to wonder what their work would be in the future. It was so exciting. Now the planet had cutting edge progress in fields that had been mysteries for centuries.

Many people losing their jobs as things were changing also had talks with the God Center. So many new jobs were being created that it was just a matter of trying something new and modifying views. The wind and solar industries grew, conversions to the new fuel sources needed people, and construction was going on everywhere on the planet. Administrations were birthed that would help immigrants assimilate to their new society; new farms were cropping up everywhere. It was a bit chaotic but sometimes changes cause chaos. Out of the chaos comes peace and harmony.

"There are over a million of our children bravely serving in this country's military. You have the best trained and experienced people with a true bent for leadership and getting things done. We have worked with your leaders, including all the Pentagon people. These forces will be used for all the rebuilding, restoration, and maintaining in this country. There is no need for a 'fighting force' no need for weapons. All military forces across the globe will be doing the same.

"The God Center has insured that this will be a planet of peace. Globally there are no fighting forces anywhere with weapons of war. Military personnel worldwide are being used for the improvements needed. The people in your military forces are a blessing by providing the manpower to fix and build things on a material basis.

"The God Center watched billions and trillions go into the Pentagon for this country's military budget. Again, this money can be used to pay off this country's debt. The 23,000 civilians and military who work in the building are all assigned management positions that will coordinate the infrastructure and new building projects going on everywhere. They are reassigned geographically throughout the 50 states to be in the center of the reconstruction. The Pentagon building will now be the home of the governmental legislators. It will become condominiums to house them while they are serving the people, and the apartments are beautiful. You will see them very soon on your media.

"There are approximately 260 working days in a year, leaving out weekends and holidays. Your legislators will be there to work as many days as the people they serve. They have already been instructed to work closely with the locals in their districts by phone and Zoom rather than taking trips 'home'. Government needs to be focused on serving as opposed to benefiting personally."

There were some conversations from Congress as they sat in their chambers resigned to cooperation.

"I had no idea I wouldn't be allowed to go home!" moaned a congressman. "And a condo in the Pentagon? I think my family will stay where they are. I'll tough it out by myself for the rest of this year and re-think a career change."

"I think it's really a better idea," said another. "We will be able to get more done, but this will all take a bit of time for this to happen."

The God Center replied directly.

"The God Center is making everything happen at once. Believe us when we tell you it was much easier to create the planet and humans in the beginning of your time than doing this makeover. Sorry but you have shown us such a total mess on Earth that we have no faith in your ability to get things done, but with our help, you will be far more organized when we leave you to your own management."

Major population centers around the planet were elated at the changes. Take India with its 189.2 million people tragically undernourished. Housing there was an abomination. As changes were shown on screens worldwide, everyone could see the stunning contrasts. The lovely people of India were joyous and dancing in the clean streets, swearing their allegiance to the God Center. Gratitude is beautiful to see.

In Africa, 257 million people were starving. Can you even imagine that number of people? Worldwide that number is 820 million hungry. Yet globally, 39% of the population worldwide is obese! A level playing field is more than a money issue. Every human being deserves proper nutrition and the God Center's control has made starvation a thing of the past.

The God Center changed governments worldwide; it wasn't just the United States. In many countries the changes were a welcomed relief since so many governments kept any and all funding for their own pleasures. The uncooperative and people the God Center knew were not going to cooperate in the future, were removed. On the whining scale however, it appeared America was a leader.

"The God Center is showing you how the world is changing before your very eyes, and you are becoming aware of the absolute awesomeness of what you are witnessing. But we are also very painfully aware that some of you are looking at changes here with a lens of fear and doubt. When you change your lens of perspective, you will see things differently and more clearly. You cannot say you have an open mind if you are wearing a lens coated in fear and doubt. You choose the way you see and respond to situations and circumstances. Change your lens, and you will be more willing to change your perspective.

"The God Center has repeatedly assured you that everything we are doing is to save you all and the planet too. Yes, it's been swift and drastic and requires adjustments in every area of life now. You can trust that everything is being done to not only save but improve living conditions across the globe.

"We are aware you have fictional stories about Utopia, with some of you laughing that it doesn't exist. We would like to correct your thinking on that as well. You have seen what we have been doing globally. Now we are going to take you on a bit of a journey, via your screens of course, to show you another planet. It was created and populated at the same time as you were, but the contrasts are stunning!

"The 'aliens' you have denied for so long do exist. You finally had to admit they exist, but you are still wrong because they are not alien. They are as human as you are, but very advanced. Their planet looks like Earth but that is about the only similarity. It concerns us that if they were to land here you would kill them. They realize that too, which is why they have not contacted you directly, but they have watched you, and their level of technology allows them to listen in to you.

"Where is your fear coming from? With a warlike mentality, anything that is different must be eliminated? Is that it? We hope that you will change your thinking and welcome the changes we have made and will continue to make.

"We have a presentation for you, complete with some interviews from the residents of Zytaria. The video will play today, please pay attention. If you ever have the opportunity to communicate with the people of Zytaria in the future, do it with a gracious attitude. If after viewing and learning about life on their planet you have questions, we will answer them. Again, please realize this "utopia" is attainable. There will be a special broadcast from our representatives in Italy later tonight. They have information on the Vatican's treasures of historical significance you won't want to miss."

Jessie arrived at the Cieslak home shortly after the broadcast concluded.

"Hi, Jessie! Come on in the living room. Logan's out in the yard but I'll let him know you're here. Just get comfy and put your books on the coffee table. Can I get you anything to drink, a lemonade or iced tea?" Patti inquired.

"That would be lovely. Whatever you're having is fine," Jessie replied, spreading her book and pictures on the table.

Patti made the drinks and called out the window to Logan that Jessie had arrived. "Be there in a minute!" he said.

"Well, that was some broadcast today, wasn't it?" Patti said, bringing a tray of lemonades into the room for the three of them.

"Yes, every day is amazing. I wanted to show you what I'm putting together. It shows a lot of what the God Center has said, about the so-called ancient aliens being here thousands of years ago. Ancient epics speak of airships and devastating wars. They speak of sky gods or star people. This isn't just in one spot but throughout the planet, like I mean everywhere. Look at this, "Jessie said pointing to pictures in one of the books she brought over. There were sketches from hieroglyphics of what was a trans-medium vehicle; it operates in multiple domains, for example in air and underwater. In other hieroglyphics were obvious spaceships.

"We definitely had visitors here. And humankind was fascinated with flight. Even boomerangs have been unearthed in Poland, Australia and Florida! That blew my mind," Jessie said.

Logan came in while Jessie was talking, grabbed lemonade from the tray and sat across from the two women in his favorite chair, scooting it up toward the coffee table.

"We don't give our ancient ancestors any credit," he said. "We've found the same tin alloy for soldering we use today in battery fragments. And we know they had electricity from all the references to 'ever burning lamps' found in their texts. This was over 2000 years ago."

"I know," Jessie replied. "They may have lived in ancient times, but it was very civilized with technologies we are only discovering ourselves. India, China, Peru and Mexico were thriving commercial centers with many cities. Some of the cities have been lost but archaeologists find new evidence of cities all the time."

"If Manuel were here, he'd tell you there is no doubt there is life on other planets. He roughly tried to estimate how many Earth sized planets might be out there. In our galaxy there are about one hundred billion stars, so there might be twenty billion earth-sized planets orbiting a sun-like star in our galaxy alone. That sounds amazing, but there are one hundred billion galaxies that we can see with our instruments. Based on that we estimate there are possibly a staggering two billion trillion planets like ours," Logan added.

"Good heavens! That many planets are possible Earths? Seriously?" Patti exclaimed.

"Yes, I'm serious. When Manuel shared that with Logan and me, we were like of course there is life out there! How could we be so arrogant as to think we are the only ones? And with all the monitoring we have done for the last few years, visits from 'the others' (I hate calling them aliens) have increased exponentially. Logan's theory of why they don't contact us is spot on. They are peace loving, we are not. We'd shoot first and ask questions later. I think once the God Center gets everyone aligned and our weapons are gone now too, well, maybe they'll be in contact with us instead of just flying over us watching."

Jessie had been leafing through a book while talking. "Now look at this – so much for our ancestors being primitive.

"The Chinese had poison gas and tear gas 2300 years before the west, and they manufactured steel from cast iron 2000 years before the west, and they even had matches in 577, a thousand years before the west. Where did this all come from? Look at their ancient texts. So many references to rockets, and visitors which of course they thought were gods. We'd think they were magicians or godlike too if we were given technologies thousands of years ahead of where we are today. Do we have anything to gain by studying the past? Plenty!"

"The book you gave me said that the 'visitors' left their calling cards everywhere; in New Mexico's Chaco Canyon, in England, Egypt, Sardina, Japan, Hawaii. These societies or cultures all say they either came from there or were visited by gods from there," Patti added.

"Yes, look here," Jessie said pointing to a picture of rock carvings. "These are deliberate designs, it's an astronomical lay out like a star mirror of the Pleiades. They mapped the stars onto the Earth. The Inca say their ancestors came from there."

"Well, I think that is what the God Center has been trying to tell people. We came from other places to evolve on Earth. Kinda funny when you think there is such a fear of aliens, when we all are," Logan laughed.

"A lot of people are pretty upset over that! Maybe if we didn't have such widespread 'creation stories' that pretty much everyone believes to a certain point anyway, it would be easier to accept this news," Patti said.

"You're right, Patti. The Inca were so progressive too. It took the Spanish Conquistadors nearly four decades of fighting with them to destroy them. And what a pity! They had such advanced knowledge I would give anything to have known all they knew," Jessie said.

"I'd like the recipe for the cement they made the pyramids out of. I would re-do the patio!" Logan said.

"What are you talking about, Logan?" Patti asked.

"According to Joseph Davidovits, the world's expert on geopolymers and man-made rocks, the stones of the pyramids were not hewn from quarries and then transported. They used rough stone and mixed it with other materials, causing a chemical process like cement. They've done tests of the stone and it is hard to tell the manufactured stone from the real stone. Egyptology disregards this. I guess they prefer the thousands of slave's stories, but those pyramids just could not have been built that way, there's no way."

"Wow, I am getting one hell of an education here. You two, it's like you have a whole other world of knowledge. I feel like a child here, with my parents telling me all these grown-up stories," Patti giggled.

"Hey girl, I've been into this for decades! And you know your husband is brilliant, what can I say?" teased Jessie.

"Brilliant? Hmm, I can't get you a raise, ya know," Logan teased her back. "But from the experiments led by Davidovits, he's demonstrated the fact that a complicated man-made geopolymeric system was produced in Egypt 4,700 years ago. Again, the fact that our ancient ancestors had such knowledge is just not something that current science can admit. Hopefully that will all change now, huh?"

"I'll leave you this book on Carnac, a village in Brittany, France you will find interesting, Patti," Jessie said. "The stones there were discovered by carbon dating to be 3000 years pre-Incan, probably the oldest site and may well be the origin of civilization. That's amazing since it was believed to have started in the Middle East."

"Wasn't that the city with the astronomical layout?" Logan inquired.

"Yes, but so many others were too. There is an almost identical layout in India, also built in about 2600 BC, so same time, and built the same too," Jessie said. "We know there had to be some kind of contact going on then because there are cities in Japan, Indonesia and South America, all with advanced knowledge that came from somewhere or someone, with each culture talking about sky gods or star people coming down to them. And another fascinating tid-bit? Many ancient civilizations used the same measuring calculations, which had to all come from the same source."

"I wish I had studied archaeology and anthropology when I was in school. I find all this so fascinating. Of course, the God Center coming down and rebooting everything is pretty damn fascinating too, isn't it?" Patti said.

"Sure is! We'll never be the same and I think that is a good thing," Jessie replied. "Other than not knowing where or what my job will be next, I'm feeling very positive about what is going on, aren't you?" Jessie asked Logan.

"Zytaria looks wonderful to me, very peaceful and organized. The housing is certainly simple, like basics without frivolity, but the gardens and parks. Wow, grab an apple for your snack as you walk through the park. Sounds good to me! To answer your question Jess, yeah, I am excited about the changes, more political than probably any other area.

"I've ranted and raved about the partisanship, all the lies, deceit, dishonesty and crap these politicians dance with. All the 'negotiating' the two parties did to get what they wanted, forgetting entirely what the people wanted. It's over! If Zytaria is any indication of what it can be like when you have a government dedicated to serving? Well, I want that," Logan said.

"I invited Manuel and Sylvia for dinner, and I hope you'll join us too, Jessie. With the Vatican news coming on later tonight, this should be a very interesting evening!" Patti said.

"Oh thanks, Patti. Sure, I would love to stay, plus I think it's good we are all together for this broadcast. I have a feeling Manuel has been through a lot with Sylvia and her family. We can offer him some support," Jessie replied.

Patti went into the kitchen to put the lasagna in the oven and started making a salad. "I'll go give Patti a hand in the kitchen," she said to Logan.

"I'll go set the table in the dining room," Logan added.

When preparations were done, the three returned to the living room. Patti was clearing up the books into a neat pile when the doorbell rang.

"Hey, Manuel and Sylvia, please come in!" Logan said ushering them into the living room. "What can I get you to drink?"

"We brought some red wine," Sylvia said, handing the bottles to Logan.

"Thanks. I'll pour you both a glass. Honey, do you want a glass of wine?" Logan asked.

"Sure, thank you. And you, Jessie?"

"Absolutely, thanks. How are you doing Sylvia?" Jessie asked as Manuel and Sylvia sat down to join them.

"It's been so hard for me, Jessie. I keep telling myself it's not just me going thru all this and that does help a little bit," Sylvia admitted.

Patti smiled. "Yes, I know what you mean, Sylvia. I had a fit at first because I hate being lied to. Once I calmed down, well Logan helped a lot with that and so has Jessie, I'm okay. We are all getting spoken to from God himself. It's really an astounding development!"

"Yes, I had to do that too! I mean, you get to the point listening to the broadcasts, that you know life is changing, God is doing it, so what use is crying and fighting it? You cannot. We just go forward," Sylvia said with a resigned tone and half-smile.

Logan appeared with a tray of wine glasses. "Let's all toast to the God Center," he offered, hoping to keep everything positive.

"I'll drink to that," Manuel said, taking his glass and clinking Sylvia's. "Here's to the God Center and getting rid of the nasty bent this country was on!"

"What are all these books you have here?" Sylvia asked.

"I've been sharing all my books and research on ancient aliens with Patti. I've been involved through travels and study on my own. Actually, I should have just stayed in college. I could have had multiple degrees by now!" she said laughing.

"Dinner's ready," Patti said. "Let's eat now before the broadcast. I'm sure tonight's information will be very enlightening."

The dinner conversations were lively with much speculation about where they would be relocated for their new jobs, also a to-be-announced issue. Praises for Patti's cooking and more wine was consumed. Patti and Jessie began to take the dinner plates into the kitchen, clearing the table, when the announcement came on.

"We will begin broadcasting from the Vatican in fifteen minutes'" was the message from the God Center.

"Oh good, then we'll have just enough time to get the dishes taken care of and make coffee to go with dessert," Patti said. "I know we don't want to miss this one."

The group of five settled in the living room for the broadcast. Patti had baked apple pie cookies, small little "pies" that are baked in a muffin tin.

"These are great!" Sylvia exclaimed. "Just like an apple pie but so easy to eat! Three bites – done! I could eat way too many of these little gems."

"Thanks! We've always loved them too. I tried peach once, but the apple seems to turn out the best."

Logan had turned the television on right after dinner, waiting, and hoping the broadcast would be visual from the Vatican. The television was showing the last rounds of a golf tournament.

"It would be nice if the broadcast could wait until all the players finish the 18th hole," Logan said.

The others laughed. "Logan, I don't think God really cares about golf," Jessie replied, still laughing.

"Golf hasn't been eliminated so it must be a god-approved activity. Oh man, did you see that putt?"

"Unreal!" Manuel said. "Hey Logan, let's go play golf tomorrow. Got anything better to do?" he asked, giving a wink to the women.

"Hmm, let's see. Left hand says clean the garage, right hand says go golfing," he had his hands palm up, raising one hand then the other like a scale measuring weights. "What to do? What a tough choice?"

"Okay, Logan. Stop the drama. Just go play golf with Manuel," Patti said while pushing both of his hand's downs.

The television went blank for a few seconds, and then an overhead shot of the Vatican appeared as the broadcast began.

"My representatives have amassed information to share with the entire world. This is being broadcast as all of our announcements have been, in every language so the world is totally included."

"First of all, the Vatican has interacted with planetary beings and possesses physical evidence of their existence. Here are pictures artifacts and old writings. From translations we performed, the humanoids from Tarku informed the leaders of the church that humans on Earth were all transplants from other planets.

"Obviously this "news" had to be hidden from all of humanity. When this happened, about 1069 AD, it caused the Vatican to have the birth of Jesus 'story' carved into a silver tablet, trying to insure the permanence of this story for all time. It had to be believed and it had to be preserved. The infallibility of the church should never be questioned and if you did question it, you were tried for blasphemy and usually eliminated. Ruling by fear never works out well.

"The famous library of Alexandria was burned to the ground in 391 AD but not before the church took what it wanted from their recorded history. All of the items of proof of extraterrestrial contact and the vast knowledge given to earthlings from other planets have been hidden in the Vatican vaults for centuries.

"Since these facts would destroy the careful plot to control people, the church had to destroy or carefully hide the truth. We have already shared with you that we sent Jesus as a messenger, not just to Earth but several other planets as well. The Virgin Birth story wasn't even written until Jesus had been dead for over fifty years. It was totally created by Paul, then relayed to Matthew and Luke who tried to give the same exact details but failed at that.

"You may have heard that there are letters in the Vatican between Nero, and Paul. This is true. They are there. Nero was not a fan of the newly emerging Christian church. Paul wrote to Nero telling him that Jesus and Mary Magdalene had a son and Paul wanted Nero to arrange safe passage for Mary and her son out of the region for their safety. Paul was not as concerned about her safety as he was being in charge himself of getting the church going. She had too many followers herself and he wanted her gone.

"Nero had the son 'accidentally' killed and shipped Mary to Gaul, which is now France.

"We know some of you suspected that the letters between Nero and Paul would either undeniably confirm the existence of Jesus as a historical person or disprove his entire existence. He did exist. He existed as a messenger. Paul was the one, in trying to convert Jews and Greeks that started calling Jesus a savior. Jesus never said he was a savior, never! He was a teacher and messenger, and he knew it. But after his death, the real creative stories began.

"Paul had studied Judaism all his life. He came from a tent-making family, well known and well off too. But he was not interested in the family business. When he tried to sell the savior idea to the Jews, who he knew thought a savior would come someday, they scoffed at him because Paul's 'savior' was dead and couldn't save anyone.

"Most of your true biblical scholars here already know that the New Testament wasn't written by the apostles, since most were fishermen and illiterate. The three epistles of John, for instance, were written by a person who simply called himself "the Presbyter". That is something that a disciple of Jesus would not have written. Apart from James, nothing in the New Testament was even written by the apostles. Illiterates cannot write.

"Another finding we can show you is the coziness between the Vatican and the Nazi's. Did you not think it odd that the Vatican never denounced the Nazi's? Pope Pius XII refused to condemn the German invasion of Poland. There were over a thousand Jews taken from Italy, right under the Pope's nose, sent by train to Auschwitz with no intervention from the Pope. The Vatican was comfortable with dictators, not democracy. Jews being killed? They weren't Catholic, were they?

"The Vatican bank, rumored to be a hidden money laundering operation, truly is and to the tune of billions. We found treasures in a vault, which are the Vatican's 'cut' of all the treasure taken from the Jews. There are 70,000 treasures in the Vatican's possession, yet on 'display' they only have 20,000.

'Their own bookkeeping shows massive profits from gold, art and valuables it hid for the Nazi's. And there is substantial paperwork showing how the Vatican arranged for Nazi's to flee to Brazil and Argentina when the war was over. It was known then as "the ratline" and it helped Nazi and Fascist war criminals' escape.

"The hatred of 'the others' generated by the bloody Crusades never stopped. The silence of the Pope during the extermination of the Jews is an inescapable fact.

"Between the lies, the double standards, manipulations and deceptions, the history we have revealed reads like a crime syndicate, rather than the 'holy' church.

"My representatives on the ground are carefully cataloging all items in the hope that every piece can be returned to its rightful owner, or family. There are massive halls filled with statuary and treasures from Egypt. Those, too, will be taken to their rightful places. This hoard of treasures, begotten illegally, is mortifying to the God Center and we are most happy to completely do away with every and all bits of this nonsense masquerading as something 'God endorsed'.

"We are sorry that so many of our children were denied the truth for so long. Looking at the history of other religions, we find their histories included stories from the star people, or sky gods. People considered them to be myths from ancient days. But there was no hiding history. Comparatively, your holy apostolic church fabricated everything to have power over the people.

"We like to keep things simple and unified. There will be no more organized religion. You are spiritual beings having a human experience. Spiritual centers, not dogma-related church buildings, will be where you can congregate. There are already wonderful, yet small congregations of spiritual people. Those will grow and expand. We will give you an updated set of commandments, expecting that you will adhere to them. We, the God Center, have saved you from an unspeakable ending. You're welcome."

Subtracting your dependence on some of the things you take for granted increases your independence. It's liberating forcing you to rely on your own ability rather than your customary crutches.

Twyla Tharp
(The Creative Habit)

DAY FIVE

Kathleen Parker, a famous Hollywood actress, woke up to find out she was not alone. Beside her, but still sleeping, was Wyatt Goodwin, the producer on her last film.

As she looked at his peaceful face, she remembered the previous evening with a gasp. He had proposed to her. But then they'd both been pretty drunk. Maybe he hadn't? The video yesterday of that planet and their way of life there scared the crap out of both of them. Things were changing too fast and neither of them knew how life would be after all this.

"Wyatt, Wyatt, wake up!" She tossed her silk pillow at him and got out of bed. The king-size bed was a cloud of white silk. The sheets, comforter, flowing bed skirts, all were the softest, most expensive bed dressings money could buy. The wall of floor-to-ceiling windows overlooking the pool and the mountains in the distance were dressed like the bed in white flowing silk draperies. Pure luxury.

"Shit! What time is it?" he moaned.

"It doesn't matter what time it is. We have a lot to talk about. I'm going downstairs to make a pot of coffee after a quick shower," she said, standing next to the bed after a whole-body stretch.

Kathleen had grown up in Hollywood. She was in her late forties and in her opinion, she was in need of some "work". She paused, staring at her face in the mirror with the pale blue eyes that were a part of her fame. *It's time*, she thought. *The eyes need to be lifted.*

"Come on," Wyatt said as he entered the bathroom. "Get in the shower with me!"

They heard the broadcast starting as they were drying off a few minutes later. "Hurry downstairs, I don't want to miss any announcements," she said grabbing her robe off the door hook and running downstairs.

"Good morning to all my children! Now that you have seen Zytaria, we are making a list of your questions about it and sending it to Zytaria. We want you to hear the citizens answer the questions personally. That broadcast will be available later today. In the meantime, we have much more to tell you about today.

"One of the big box stores enjoyed over $400 billion last year in income, and they will be graciously (our choice of words because we always take a positive spin on things) contributing to the criminal justice system across the United States and contributing to the national debt elimination funds. This funding of the justice system will allow for more education and training for police officers, streamlining the entire court system, and releasing those incarcerated wrongly. The God Center knows who these people are. It will also temporarily supply funding for prisons and jails until such time as they can be either modified or eliminated altogether.

"With 80 percent of their products at these big box stores, as you call them, coming from China, they will be adjusting their business to only offer Made In USA products. The God Center is bringing manufacturing back here, where it belongs. This is the end of outsourcing to another country. This is a perfect example of greed. Companies wanted more profits and cheaper foreign labor was their plan. Since profits are capped now, any excess profit goes into a special fund called *"Help"*. It will be used wherever funds are needed. Think of this as a savings account for emergencies.

"Now all manufacturing is here for everything you need right here in your own country. There is no more outsourcing by your manufacturers. You have the room, the people and the necessary resources. Importing and exporting needed balance. If you truly want to be as great as you are capable of being, you should not have to rely on the labor of other countries for products previously manufactured right here. Self-sufficiency is powerful. Every country is being restructured to provide a decent level of self-sufficiency. Importing/Exporting will be done on a need basis, not profit.

"Oil companies, who have profits of hundreds of billions, are being phased out almost entirely. The God Center brought technology that makes gasoline for cars obsolete. The people in the oil industry will move right into producing the new fuels, with a modest profit unlike the present. Any profits can be used for either expansion or sharing with every employee of the company. The days of CEO's making fortunes is so over.

"The God Center hears that many of you are still not sure about the changes here. We do have something really fun to tell you. Thanks to the just a bit of money from the oil industries, Disneyland, and all the large amusement parks will be of no cost to you! There! Have fun, our children. Play and play nice. The industry making a large contribution to the Earth's pollution, and also making insane profits, is now taking charge of fun. Isn't that great? See? We do love you!"

Back in Washington, legislators had been watching the twenty-four-hour viewing of changes around the world. The God Center knew that there were hearts and minds not quite in the right place yet with a few of them.

The viewing of Zytaria blew minds. It was so radically different from anything on Earth. Many wondered if the God Center intended for Earth to copy Zytaria?

"I know what I'm seeing is some kind of miracle," said the senator from South Carolina. "I just don't know if I trust what I'm seeing. I sure don't believe that Zytaria is real."

"I think you'd better believe it! It will be a whole new Earth when the pods leave." said his assistant Mike.

"Oh, see? You aren't saying it's God – it's when the pods leave to you?

"Senator, changes are being made worldwide, like in an instant!" Mike said pleadingly, knowing the senator's anger for these past few days had been volatile.

"Yes, I see that. But my life will never be the same! My money has all but disappeared, I'm now working for $300 a week for Christ's sake, I just lost millions, millions, do you understand?"

"You aren't alone. It's the same for many." Mike added.

"Well, it's just not right. Some kind of Indian-giver! I made millions only to have it taken away from me and given to some poor slob without front teeth!" he raged. "I'm reconsidering. I don't want to see whatever hippy dippy world this is going to be!"

With that statement, the senator's hand went up. He was removed.

It was not uncommon for some to check themselves out. It was the one thing the God Center was sad about. Always keeping the common good as the priority, there is always a contingent of naysayers, of belligerence, of anger that would have to be eliminated. The God Center wanted this to be a choice, a voluntary self-removal, but the God Center was also removing people who showed absolutely no heart connection to the Higher Power, let alone understanding the "for the common good" approach. If the previous days of lectures and now actually seeing the global improvements had not convinced some, what else would?

Listening to the comments about Zytaria being a socialist world brought out such anger. Earth was a mix of the "have's" and the "have nots", with the former having all the power and control over the latter. Obviously the "have's" were not taking this well.

"Things are changing rapidly, and the God Center is well pleased. Before, it was the people with the least who sacrificed the most. Now it's the people with the most who are going to sacrifice the most. The greediest among you are split in your reactions. Half of you are accepting this re-appropriation of fortunes, even with a modicum of pleasure knowing they will really be helping the world. The other half is mumbling things like the following:

"What is this kumbaya crap?"

"This is communism in disguise."

"I've lost everything. This can't be God!"

"Others have been asking to be removed. While the God Center is saddened by these attitudes and choices, we continue to see the bigger picture of a thriving planet, just minus a few players. Well, to be honest, thousands on Earth have chosen to leave. And we are watching some people who were involved with conflicts and wars. Weapons are gone but we know what is in the heart and mind of everyone. We will remove more before our God Center pods leave.

"We heard some of your younger people say that we are God casts, like your podcasts. We like that. We have a Godcast! Cute! We also heard some of you saying we didn't 'speak like God'.

"One wonders why you would say that. We speak exactly like you do in order to communicate easily with you. You want us to speak with an accent? Y'all think we can't? We know every language on the planet! OMP, drop all your judgments and criticisms. Your hubris is embarrassing! Do you even realize you are critiquing your God, your Source? Be kind!

"The God Center wants you to know, that although some in your government have requested removal, the Party of the People, or POP (we love that!) is working very well together with the assignments they have been given. We are confident the remaining legislators will be working for you! They have no one else to answer to and no sources of additional income now. This government works for the people, all of the people.

"Importantly, we have chosen people on local levels that are dispersing those 'extra' funds to those in need. Housing, food, health care and transportation are being given to all. We have done countless miracles in some parts of your cities and rural areas. We made massive improvements in Africa, India and South America, which you have witnessed on your screens.

"How sad to see people in America living in shacks, some without electricity, running water, and with little food at all. Then, by stark contrast, CEO's making millions, with two of them having space races that cost billions. OMP! We'll 'Godcast' some of the recipients for you all to see pure joy and sincere gratitude. Look at it! See the tears of relief and happiness for thousands of you! Watch this and as you watch, realize you could have helped them yourselves. We hope you will see that giving is better than getting and, in the future, if you have more than you need, do not hoard it. Give it away. It will multiply and grow. With the spirit of gratitude, more is given!"

"Wow, I'll bet there are a lot of pissed off millionaires, huh? Carl said, while having breakfast with his pregnant wife, Katie. They lived outside of Atlanta in a modest three-bedroom home with their golden-doodle, Henry.

"Frankly, I'm glad this is happening," Katie said. "Who needs that much money to live on anyway?"

Carl chuckled. "Well, it's the way they live that costs so much. But you're right. You would be hard pressed to spend it all. Oh sure, there are plenty of folks calling themselves philanthropists, giving millions to charities, but if you can give millions, just how much money do you have anyway? And what the hell are you doing with it?"

Katie nodded in agreement. "To live a decent life doesn't take all that much if you're not extravagant. I see that kind of extravagance going bye-bye. At first, I thought I would be sad about so much being taken away from us. But when you realize, even though you and I are middle class, there were millions of people with absolutely nothing. That breaks my heart so you can imagine how God felt about that, huh?"

"Well, that's just one reason the God Center is here," Carl remarked. "I'm thinking of the future for our child, Katie, and I want to believe that with all the restructuring going on, it will be a better place to raise kids. Big changes at work, which really needed to be made. I'm relieved not to be in charge of manufacturing the crap we were."

Carl was a purchasing agent for one of the largest food manufacturers. One of their hottest selling items was a box of macaroni and cheese that you could cook yourself, just add milk and butter. The people buying this product didn't realize it was made with chemicals that "tasted like" cheese, when in fact no cheese was in the box. Carl was the one buying the ingredients. It made him sick to think about the people consuming this product. And there were others, all prepackaged convenience foods, all devoid of nutrition but people loved the taste. The chemists in the labs for this company were masters of trickery and even better at adding the chemicals that make their products addictive.

Carl's company was being restructured; the manufacturing end will be making pasta, plain pasta. All "flavoring laboratories" were being eliminated. Natural flavors would be the only additives going forward.

In an office in downtown Manhattan, there was chaos. The CEO and upper management came out of the conference room where tempers had flared.

"We can't just fire everyone. There is still work to do, isn't there?" Shelly asked.

"Work? What work? Our factories are being retrofitted with all new equipment, to make new products. We don't even know what we are supposed to do! I just lost millions, and God only knows what is next!" Phil Martin, CEO shot back.

"You're right. God does know." Shelly replied.

With that, the God Center turned on. "We are giving you a layout of what this company will be and an operation plan for you to follow. We understand that the changes are coming faster than anyone can adjust to and we ask your patience. This is a global operation. How do you go about prioritizing the entire planet?

"We know your story of how we made the Earth and everything on it in six days. Believe us that was easier than cleaning up here now! We actually did it, the whole creation, in three days, just for the accurate record. You managed to complicate even the simplest of things. We are asking for your cooperation and that means being patient as we work together. We know every detail about your business so explaining and re-training will be all that is needed right now."

Phil was shocked that the God Center was listening. It is a hard concept to get used to, like Big Brother watching over you all the time, but it was necessary to communicate with as many individuals as possible.

In a mansion on Long Island, tempers flared.

"Go to hell, Bill! I'm tired of your excuses!" Jill shouted.

"It's not an excuse. The money is GONE I'm telling you. You are not going to Paris fashion week."

"Honestly, you believe those aliens! You're a dumb ass, Bill."

"Have you not heard a word the God Center has said? Have you not watched the Godcast and witnessed the miraculous changes going on all over this planet? Don't call me a dumb ass, Jill! You were never the brightest crayon in the box, but now you are just being stupidly childish!"

"You are so mean to me! I'll be leaving to talk to my lawyer. I will get your damn money, all of it. You wait and see!" she screamed on her way out of the house.

Bill sat at his desk. It was a gorgeous carved piece of furniture, placed just right to take in the view out of the palatial windows to the manicured English gardens below. He sat holding his head in his hands, feeling his loss. Jill could not see, would not see, the future. He smirked to himself, "There goes my trophy wife, pretty little thing, but do women come dumber than she is?"

Bill was typical of a lot of executives. They literally were their jobs. Without them, without their sense of wealth and power, they were going through a major identity crisis that few could withstand. Bill was hardly the only one who, after a few moments alone in his expansive and expensive home office, seriously considered raising his hand for removal.

The Godcast continued.

"We are hearing all of your financial experts and some in POP who are saying there is not enough money to improve the living conditions of the poor. Please stop concerning yourselves. We would not be here doing this if we didn't know in advance that this is a planet of plenty!

"Your Forbes magazine said there are some 21 trillion dollars in offshore bank accounts. They weren't even close! We found 114 trillion. That is quite enough to level the playing field. And for those of you having hissy fits over taxes, we have streamlined taxes, social security and investments. You will have to refrain from the 'I'm so screwed' train of thought and move into 'Look at how we can live together in harmony.' Remember people, challenges are always opportunities for growth! Everyone and anyone that needs help are getting it. Everyone.

"Just to reiterate, you are all children of the God Center. No one race is better than the other, despite how you have treated one another. This marks the absolute end of any discrimination whatsoever. If you are so bent on believing otherwise, please raise your hand. We do not tolerate the slightest discrimination. If people around, you start 'disappearing' this will be why.

"Hey, have you seen that bumper sticker that says, 'God don't make no junk!' That's correct, not the English part but the statement itself. We made all of you just as you are. We thought diversity was a good thing, and having different cultures was a good thing so you could all contribute to society in different areas. That was the plan. It worked on other planets, as you have seen for yourselves with the video from Zytaria.

"We don't expect to copy everything on Zytaria here, but you are being given the opportunity to re-boot some of the uglier thinking. Now equality is being enforced since you couldn't seem to get there by yourselves. We know your hearts, and thoughts so if you think for a minute, you'll just keep quiet for now until we are 'gone' you are dead wrong! You may not have the silver orbs grid covering the planet, but the God Center is always monitoring everything, everywhere."

Mark had lived on the streets for a year and a half. He wasn't a bum. He lost his wife to a horrendously long and expensive battle with cancer. They had mortgaged themselves beyond what they should have had to pay for her treatments. He'd missed so much work taking care of her that he'd lost his job and sometime after she died, he'd lost his home. Mark never imagined at 48 he would be on the street after a lucrative career, yet here he was.

He was living in his car in a parking lot full of other homeless who still had their cars. Uninsured, his blue Mazda SUV housed all that he had left. Some clothes, books, two blankets and a pillow were all that was left of his life. He had spray painted the inside of the windows so he could sleep as privately as possible. He bused tables at a nearby restaurant providing him enough money to eat. He was desperately trying to save money to get some place to live. He had nobody to help him.

The stories of the homeless ran the gamut of illnesses, drug addictions, bankruptcies and job loss. Mark was one of the typical people. Before becoming homeless himself, he would drive by areas of tents and garbage, cussing at the losers and addicts who were 'crapping up' his neighborhood. There were few people who took the time to help anyone there, let alone talk to them.

After the God Center arrived with love, compassion and help, Mark spent two nights sleeping in St. Bartholomew's church until he received the keys to his new apartment and a wallet with money for food. Everyone in the church was singing God's praises as the representative from the God Center distributed the money and keys. Jobs would be created for everyone as companies were coming back to the United States and manufacturing would once again be sustaining the country. Mark wept openly at the gift from God, as he put it.

The God Center put into motion the necessary ingredients for all countries to produce what they needed so that trade among countries would begin anew. The point was that each country maintains its own needs first and excess production could be traded. Pride in manufacturing the best quality products was revived. This applied especially to the appliance manufacturers. Cheap short cuts, built-in obsolescence and slave wages were never to be allowed again.

In Hollywood, the previously wealthy had decisions and choices thrust upon them.

Wyatt sat stirring his coffee watching Kathleen making their toasted bagels. "Did you want to get married?" he inquired of Kathleen.

"God, Wyatt. What a fucking romantic you are!" she said laughing. "Sure! Why the hell not? I can't afford this house by myself anyway."

"Oh, now you are being the romantic. But okay, I get it. My overseas investments are gone. I don't have a lot either now. Sure, let's combine whatever we have left and try to make the best of it. I do love you; you know."

"Well let's hear what's next from the Godcast." Kathleen suggested, as she brought the bagels to the table and kissed the top of Wyatt's balding head.

"Oh my people, we have witnessed small acts of irresponsibility, which if not corrected, then become larger issues. Let's take a small one, an everyday silly little thing that shows selfishness, if not irresponsibility.

"Grocery carts. The carts belong to the store you got them from, to use in their store and to transport the bags to your car. And then? Many of you just leave the cart anywhere. The carts are there for use, not abuse.

'Oh yes, we hear you. You were too tired, too in pain, you just couldn't walk anymore. Why, then, did you not ask for help? Most stores will carry your groceries out for you. Some stores have pick up areas where you leave your cart outside in the pick-up area and drive your car up to it. People should be kind enough to help you if you need it. We are sorry, but your inability to return a shopping cart is inexcusable. Ask for help in the store, or have your groceries delivered.

"Sounds cruel? It's not at all. If one person sees another leaving their cart, odds are they too will leave theirs. And so, it goes until some poor employee has to go out to the parking lot and gather up the pieces of your irresponsibility. This is basic cooperation on an everyday easy level. Ask for help if you need it with anything"

"Thank God! I've always been ticked off about that. I always thought, hey, you can walk miles in the grocery stores because they're so huge, but you can't take 50 more steps to bring the cart back?" Kathleen said.

"I think the God Center sees how damn lazy everyone is, and that's what it is despite all the excuses. And it's true the store people absolutely will help you out with your groceries. When I had a bit of a limp, left over after twisting my ankle, not a big limp, but still a limp. I asked if they could help me. That's all it takes. Just ask somebody. Man, oh man, people are too lazy to even think, because they don't think to ask for help," Wyatt said.

"You've got that right!" Kathleen replied with a laugh. "Ayn Rand said the masses were ignorant. Boy she is right about that. Imagine the level of stupidity we have dipped down to for the God Center to have to come here and teach the basics. And we've been thinking how advanced and civilized we are. What delusional thinking. I'm looking forward to a whole new Earth, aren't you?"

"Yes, I am, truly I am," Wyatt replied. "Changes yes many, but all for the common good. I never thought in a million years I'd be a witness to God coming down here to save us, but wow, this has been one holy experience!"

"Glad we didn't have to interpret some burning bushes!" Kathleen said. "There is nothing left to question anymore. All we must do is love one another, share and be kind. Pretty simple when you leave out all the struggles with trying to get ahead of the pack, trying to make more, have more, that whole vicious merry-go-round where far too many fall off. I was frightened at first, but I sure feel better now, don't you?"

"Yep, I think everything will be just fine, maybe not immediately, but we seem to be working toward a very equalized global society," Wyatt said.

Continuing with the day's broadcast the God Center touched on other things.

"How about following driving rules? Use your turn signals and do not speed! The limits were set for your safety. The God Center has witnessed what you call road rage. Breathe people, just calm down.

"Judgments here on this planet must end. There is absolutely nothing to be gained by judging another person. You are different, true, but that is not a bad thing, as it was our intention. Do not forget that you are all children of God. If you don't like someone because their personality is too silly, or too serious, or whatever 'vibe' you want to avoid, just let them be. You don't need to talk about them as if they are bad, just because you have a problem with them. Nobody is perfect and believe us, you all came from the same place. Honor diversity and be kind.

"The God Center witnesses so much anger and impatience on this planet. This is a lot of ego out of control. If your thoughts are negative thoughts of irritation, anger, impatience or even sadness, becoming aware of this is a good start. If you complain about yourself, how useless you are, just listen to yourself and your thoughts. Thoughts become things. Once you have awareness, you are at the beginning of freedom from the ego. Love yourselves as God's creation. Truly if you don't love yourself, you cannot give love to anyone else. It starts with you! You cannot give out what you do not have inside. Love yourselves, and then you have love to give others.

"If there is a need to change something, like losing weight, becoming a better cook, getting more education, this is the time to start. Stop with all the very creative excuses and decide! This is not a dress rehearsal.

"We've been intrigued with a game everyone plays called the Blame Game. Blaming your parents, friends, spouses, the government, the weather, oh my, the list is endless. Using whatever is in your personal history as an excuse to be mean (I was abused), to being an alcoholic (I was mistreated or it runs in the family), or to think pity is deserved for your history, stop blaming. Look at today. It is a new beginning. Leave the past behind and get on the love-one-another train. Each one of you is your own train engine. Love your engine and go forward. Leave your stinky garbage behind and start anew.

"Many of you have just lost your jobs. Can you describe what happened without judgment? What happened – job loss – simply means you do not currently have a job. But you will look for another one. It is hardly the end of the world. We are in charge of the end of the world, remember? And we have made the decision to save you all from yourselves and rescue this planet."

"There are some excellent teachers among you that can help. Eckhart Tolle is a favorite, and Maryann Willliamson, as well as the spiritual writings of Yanhao Huang, Wayne Dyer, and Ernest Holmes. You know reading is great for your brain. Do acquaint yourselves with these people and sincerely work on being the best that you can be with whatever you choose to do. The God Center wants you all to thrive, but you cannot continue ego-driven, selfish or irresponsible behaviors. Kindness Rules!

"You want to know what to believe in? Believe in love. Believe in sharing. Believe in helping others. Know contentment. Take a few moments to think about what we are telling you."

"I suppose we should live in your house?" Wyatt asked Kathleen.

"Absolutely. I don't think anyone could afford to buy your house, Wyatt. You paid twelve million or so for it. I can't imagine what it will sell for now with the 'level-the-playing-field' program we're being dealt," Kathleen said quietly.

She knew Wyatt had lost his fortune. But he was a good man, very kind and respectful. She had done much worse in the past she knew. Wyatt was balding but his physique was pretty good for a man in his 50's. His height of 6'4" had him towering over Kathleen at 5'4" but they looked good together. Kathleen was forever in a battle with her weight because in Hollywood ten extra pounds could eliminate you from a role you coveted. She would never be the tall slender person on the outside that she dreamed of being.

"Hell, they can make it into condos for all I care anymore. With twelve bedrooms and fourteen bathrooms, really, Kathleen, what was I thinking?"

"You had too much money, Wyatt!" Kathleen teased. "You did what we all did in Hollywood. We bought as much as we could to prove to ourselves, we'd made it. We had it all. Great fun while it lasted, right?"

"Yes, it was! But it was selfish when you see what has been on our screens from the God Center. I knew poverty existed. I just didn't know how bad it really was! I want to get some of the books the Godcast spoke about. Have you read any of them?"

"No, but I've heard of them. Now is a good time I suppose. Let's go down to the bookstore when this Godcast is over." Just as she spoke, the broadcast continued.

The God Center heard them and replied, "We are sending representatives to your Hollywood area, and several other areas with multi-million-dollar homes. Thank you both for seeing that equalization is not a bad thing.

"Our reps will work with mansion owners to convert the homes into communal family complexes, if they have extended families. Homes with excessive bedrooms can accommodate large families. All the 'values' will be adjusted to reflect the 'adjusted' incomes people will have now. We already have a large family for your home, Wyatt and you will receive compensation for it, though it won't be twelve million, sorry."

The Godcast continued for everyone.

"Bigger, better, best – the constant human desire to have more, have the best of everything is a very strong mindset with humans here. If something will benefit the common good – like wanting a mailbox on your corner, that's fine. To pine away or whine away because you desire a new car, when there is nothing wrong with what you have is not being content. The human need to want more needs to be channeled away from just you, the individual, to all people.

"After viewing Zytaria, you know there are many civilizations, created in tandem with yours, on other planets far more advanced than you are. Do you know why? They have a history, the very beginning of which was very similar to yours here on Earth. There were wars, persecutions, and land grabs for power and control. However, when the messengers arrived to teach them peace, love, sharing and decency, they listened. They didn't kill the messengers, oh no, they changed their ways.

"Everything on their planets revolves around cooperative generosity and keeping the whole, the common good, their priorities. They have not wasted treasure on wars as in their past, they have not created a myriad of religion clubs, they have not frittered away their finances and they have no greed. Just think of what Earth would be like without just those four things? Uniting yourselves right now is critical to sustain humanity and the planet.

"We would be incomplete in our renovation of Earth if we did not address your holidays. We understand the addiction to the

154

commercialism of Christmas as well as the prior religious reasons. An industry evolved from this love of Christmas – decorations, cards, overspending on presents, all to the tune of one trillion dollars.

"One trillion dollars annually to celebrate a day, just one day? People go into debt buying stuff because wow, it's Christmas! This holiday has evolved from the simplest of traditions, the majority of which are pagan customs. A rather remarkable adaptation, wouldn't you agree?

"And who were the pagans? Anyone from the early Romans to the Norse in Scandinavia, who were not Christians. Christian missionaries swarmed Europe in the early AD's and as they did, they learned of varying religious systems and beliefs. All these people and religions were lumped into the catch-all word "pagan" by the early Christians. It was the Christian plan to rule the world either by total conversions or total destruction. The Christians however were fascinated by some of the traditions and picked up a few of them here and there. The date of Christmas itself coincided with Winter Solstice. As long as the church incorporated other traditions, they were considered sanctified, thereby acceptable. Anything or anyone who deviated in the slightest was killed."

As the Godcast continued, many people listening were having a hard time with the elimination of Christmas. So much was changing so fast. Truths were coming out daily, wiping out many traditions on Earth. The God Center had to explain how Earth had gone off the rails, knowing people would balk and holler, yet changes had to be made.

"The Winter Solstice was a huge part of the pagan life. They were primarily agricultural people, and winter marked the end of the year's harvest and the chance to celebrate with loved ones as they rested from the work in the fields.

"The gift giving came from the Romans who exchanged small gifts for the sake of good luck for the bountiful harvest in the next year. This has morphed into what you have now, a multi-million-dollar business.

"Santa Claus is a mishmash of the generous St. Nicholas and the gods Odin and Sleipnir. Again, stories and traditions are over-blended. The Christmas tree decorating has origins with the Romans and early Germanic tribes who honored the god Odin throughout the winter solstice. So, the tree you spend time and money on is to celebrate a god you know nothing about which is unbelievable. To cling so much to a tradition is sad when you know nothing of Odin.

"Caring about the history and origins of traditions has been ignored and what little history you know about has been twisted to make this holiday over the top. Take all of this, add your slogan of Jesus is the Reason, and everything done is justified? Let us assure all of you, Jesus would be absolutely appalled the way his supposed birth is celebrated. Can you not see this? How you can claim someone like him as your savior and yet ignore what he really tried to teach you is astounding! Christmas here as the God Center sees it is pure man-made hypocrisy. It has nothing to do with Jesus, who if he saw what you were doing for this holiday, he would knock down your Christmas tree just as he cleared the temple of those who were more focused on money than God.

"There are pitifully few people who help the poor at this time of year. They are too concerned about their decorated house being the envy of all, their children getting whatever their little heart's desire even though they go into debt for it and on and on. More than half the population cannot afford to celebrate Christmas the way it has evolved which is outrageous. Out of the 200 countries on your planet, 40 do not celebrate it at all. And Earth is the only planet doing this trillion-dollar extravagance. Listen to us. The only planet! This is not universal by any means. It has been created and evolved into a money-centered waste on your planet.

"The material things aren't the point of a holiday. Better to be grateful for the gifts of family, friends, your health, food on the table, and memories. There is no cost to sharing presence, as opposed to presents. Life is about people, not stuff.

"There is absolutely no reason to continue this craziness. Instead, use January 1st as a day of significance. If you insist on saving your decorations, use them then, but it's all so unnecessary. Hopefully as people adjust, the decorating will be on a much smaller scale. Limits of one gift each will make it special and not drive people into lunacy shopping and enduring debts just so there are piles of presents under the pagan tree celebrating an ancient god. Materialism has been like a drug on this planet.

"Celebrating on January 1st starts your calendar year with whatever prior Christmas tradition you wish to carry forward but eliminate the word Christmas. Perhaps Renewal Day or whatever you choose. You can vote with your new government representatives what to call the January 1st holiday. Please don't renounce the use of reason.

"This planet has more celebratory events annually than virtually any other planet, yet another way Earth stands out. All of the inhabitants in other worlds are far superior in accomplishments and progress because they do not waste their money and energy the way people on Earth do.

"Lewis Carroll said *One of the deep secrets of life is that all that is really worth doing is what we do for others.*' So bring that into your celebrations. Rather than being caught up in overabundance and frivolity, do something significant for someone in need. No matter how we try to level your playing field, there is always going to be someone who needs help. Find them! Help them!

"I have just this minute received the connection from Zytaria with answers to your questions about life on their planet. Here is the transmission on your screens."

The screen showed a picture of several people sitting at a table in a garden, two women and two men, "normal looking" humans.

A woman with long straight blonde hair spoke first with a bit of an accent, possibly German.

"Hello, my name is Katya. You asked if abortions are legal or illegal. The answer is neither. We do not interfere with anyone's medical decisions. It is personal. It is between God and the woman involved. It is very strange to think your government is involved in such a private matter. Another question about dental services being free as well as medical? Yes, it is.

"Another earthling wanted to know about shopping. We have stores here to buy clothes of course. We have seen your shopping stores, or malls. We do not have anything that extravagant. Clothing is priced uniformly throughout Zytaria. We have good quality and a variety of designs that are affordable to all. Those people on Zytaria who love textiles and color, have received the best education to produce their designs but we do not have 'designer' clothing that costs a fortune. That would be unfair. Many women on Zytaria, and a few men as well, know how to sew and some make their own clothing. Thank you for your questions." she said with a smile.

The next speaker was male, with red curly hair and a mustache framing his big smile and a Scotish brogue. "Hello earthlings! My name is Blair. You have asked about cars here. They are not like yours, but we do have vehicles for personal transport. Most of our vehicles are the size of your Volkswagen beetles but they are all battery operated. We have larger vehicles used only for vacations or moving. They hold up to 12 people when used for travel. They have expansion capability to transport a house full of possessions when people move. Someone asked if we have car racing here. No, we do not.

"We have excellent monorails here, so it is not necessary to use private transport for everything. We do have bicycles like yours on Earth, and some have battery power. Most of all, people on Zytaria enjoy walking as much as possible. It is good for our health.

"My last question to answer is what your divorce rate is? First of all, we do not have a "marriage", we have agreements. It is suggested that we live together for a minimum of a year before agreeing to stay together. If we plan to have children, we then take a pledge in a ceremony with our families attending. We pledge to raise our children together. Divorce is not common here, only .02% of the population ever divorces, although we call it cancellation of the pledge, not divorce. We appreciate your questions and your interest in Zytaria."

The camera then moved to an Oriental man whose smile was glowing as he greeted the viewers. "Hello to you on Earth! My name is Linsu. We are so pleased to tell you about our world. And we are so happy the God Center has chosen to save the Earth. Some of you want to know if the God Center has ever visited us. Not in the way that is happening on your planet.

"We have an intimate relationship with Source through our meditation centers and personal meditation. What is happening on Earth was not necessary here. Yes, in our history we had power grabs and greed, but messengers from the God Center came here and explained that Source was unhappy with this, that we needed love and harmony. It took us nearly a century to work with the visitors who were teaching us physics, geometry, astronomy, and advanced engineering and mathematics.

They came to Earth too, as emissaries from the God Center. We benefited from the technologies they brought us and decided to leave our warring behind and go with the love, peace and harmony. There is no one on this planet that would ever regret this or want to go back to the way it was here. We in Zytaria believe you will make the transition to a loving and cooperative planet. It has been an abrupt change for all of you, but your lives will be more fulfilling and peaceful going forward.

"You also asked if we ever visited Earth. Yes. We have been visiting for quite some time. A few of us lived among you for a while from time to time. We had to assimilate ourselves so you would not realize we were what you call 'aliens' since you tend to attack anything you find different. We are taught non-judgment here, so let's just say I personally was very glad to come home to Zytaria. The racial prejudice on Earth was intolerable. I can't imagine living with that.

"We will cheer you on with the changes you are making! And we look forward to your joining our planetary friends. Thank you for your questions."

The camera went next to a lovely woman with very black skin, showing the versatile races on Zytaria. She too had a beautiful smile and very bright shiny eyes. All the respondents appeared very happy.

"Greetings, from Zytaria! My name is Amana. We are so happy to be sharing information with you in the knowing you will soon join our friendly corner of the universe! A question that I was given to respond to was how do we treat depression on Zytaria? We aren't sure what that is. We may have moments of sadness, but it doesn't last. We can always talk with our spiritual specialists, spend time in the meditation center, or go to the park. If, for some reason, the sadness hangs around, we have herbs that help. It is rare to have sadness that lasts. We have a beautiful world. We have contentment here that we have not seen much of on Earth. When you are content, sadness will rarely visit.

"The other question I was given is do we miss holidays? We have 6 weeks of holidays a year, so what are we missing? Holidays are meant for fun, travel, parties, and we have festivals of art, music and theater all the time. We have fun here, so we are not missing anything.

"We have seen your holidays. All I can say is be happy to save your money. It will be wonderful to see your planet peaceful and prosperous. We look forward to visiting soon so hold love in your hearts for one another. We send love to all of you! Thank you."

The last respondent speaking was a man with black braids in his hair, kind loving eyes and warm smile.

"Hello, my special friends! My name is Alois. I am so grateful to tell you more about Zytaria. A question was about wealth. How are people motivated to work if not for accumulating wealth and getting ahead?

"Ahead of what, exactly? I know it is not proper to answer a question with a question. And yet, this concept is not one we have here. We are all happy to work because we all contribute to the lives we live here. Our educational system allows us to sample prospective occupations at an early age and we can change occupations whenever we feel compelled to do so. When you are happy doing what you are doing, it makes all the difference. Everyone's service makes our society run smoothly. There were a few people who asked questions about this possibly being a dictatorship or authoritarian. Nothing could be more opposite. Our government serves the people.

"If the people ask for changes, the changes are made. We do not see a problem with this. We are not controlled by a government, by a religion, by anything except the rules of the God Center. The government serves us, we serve the God Center. It is simple here. We do not have all the procedural paths; we do not have complicated anything really.

"We here at Zytaria hope that the changes to your own government will help you evolve and progress the way the God Center desires. We send love to you all!"

The God Center returned to the broadcast.

"We hope that seeing your family on Zytaria gives you whatever reassurances you may need to feel good about the changes we are making here. You see them on their planet, happy, well-adjusted, and peaceful. We didn't select only happy people to talk to you; they all are. They have less nonsense and more common sense. This is what the God Center had hoped would happen here. It didn't on its own, but here we are, to save you from yourselves.

"We were speaking of your holiday traditions when the Zytaria connection came through, so let us finish."

"Thanksgiving, oh it sounds so worthy, doesn't it? No need for it. Save that turkey for a Sunday dinner. No reason to have a day off or to spin this into the Black Friday shopping frenzy. Your history stories are mostly in error anyway. The pilgrims you think are so holy committed genocide. Gratitude should begin every day in your heart and mind. Try it!

"As for an Easter celebration? Celebrate your <u>own</u> Resurrection! Rise up and away from your erroneous historical stories. Again, it's a mishmash of religion stories and an Easter bunny? More candies, decorations and whatnot are for a grand total 21.6 billion dollars on another holiday? It's incomprehensible, isn't it? Do not wonder why we are eliminating this one. Common sense!

"If you want to celebrate something in the spring, have a Spring Day – celebrate it however you want to without spending money. It is a challenge, isn't it? According to your climates, spring is at different times of the year, so make it a local celebration. First Sunday in May for the North American continent would be perfect. Work with your state representatives for setting up some fun, be it sports, music, planting your gardens or having art fairs. Celebrating should not cost billions.

"In like manner, the first Sunday of July can be a summer celebration, eliminating the Fourth of July. The fireworks terrorize all the animals on the planet who certainly do not enjoy it. Respect them please. They were all created with the same unlimited love you were created from. Live together in peace and harmony.

"This brings up another issue, animal abuse. We bless those of you who rescue animals from deplorable conditions. We know the rest of you claim to 'feel sorry' for them, and yet you have no pity for the animals in the CAFO's? All animals are considered sacred by the God Center, just as you are. You will find a commandment that includes reverence for all life, including animals, in the announcements when we depart."

Patti and Logan were sitting on their patio listening, sipping iced teas. "There isn't much that isn't being changed or eliminated is there?" she said.

"That's for sure. But I'll tell you, I'm blown away at the collective cost of what we have made of some of these holidays. I had no clue, did you?"

"Of course not. But if you added up what everyone spends, while individually it doesn't seem like much, the total is rather mind blowing," Patti said, thinking back to when the boys were little. Easter baskets, special outfits for church, and decorations all cost money.

"This is sure a wakeup call for the ways where we have evolved into a very extravagant society. I never thought about it really. Remember how everyone commented that the Satori's down the street who are Buddhist ignored our holidays? Our neighborhood seemed to think they were freaks. Kind of a laugh now, isn't it? They had it right all along," Logan smirked.

"I was just writing in my journal about the life changes yesterday. At first, I was all teary-eyed thinking of what we supposedly were losing. Then I turned that thought around to what we would be gaining by simplifying our lives and all I could feel was gratitude," Patti said.

"That's beautiful, honey. Yes, we will be recreating things and once you get past what we are losing, it is exciting to think of how much better off everyone will be. And I don't mean just you and I, but the entire planet," Logan replied. "Couldn't you just see the peace and happiness on the faces of the Zytarians? Talk about contentment! I want that, don't you?"

Butterflies hovered over Patti's flower garden; birds were singing and dipping down to the myriad of bird feeders Patti kept filled. The patio spanned the width of the house and had several large planters overflowing with flowers. Patti loved nature and created a garden she called 'sacred'. It was her favorite place to write in her journal, surrounded by nature. The years she spent orchestrating this garden, sweating, digging, arranging, all paid off. The thought of having to relocate with Logan made her feel a bit sad. She was trying to practice gratitude for everything while struggling to accept the fact that they may move.

Logan sensed this. "Honey, I promise you, wherever we go, we will make a garden like this one," and he reached for her hand across the redwood table and gave it a squeeze.

The broadcast continued.

"Halloween is horrid and filled with candy junk that everyone is expected to buy for kids who rarely say thank you. Done. Gone. Do you realize this is an eight-million-dollar holiday? Money spent on decorations, costumes and candy is frivolous. Some of the poorer communities struggled with this, having no money to participate. It was so bad that some schools had to eliminate costumes in schools that day because there were so many who could not afford them. How tragic and how absolutely unnecessary. Plus, the sugar, oh my people, you are killing yourselves slowly with sugar. Candy, candy, candy and you wonder why this planet is full of sickness! Learn about nutrition and give up the sugar except for maybe a small treat now and then, but not daily.

"In lieu of this, have Imagination Day and let the kids choose some book or movie character to dress as and make parties in your homes with treats. Horrors being celebrated? Being scared by terrifying costumes and haunted houses? Fright seems more revered here than contentment. There is no other planet wasting so much time and money, and all in the name of what? Fun? No more of this, including door-to-door seeking candies, which was becoming very dangerous anyway on Earth.

"Valentine's Day was a good one for Hallmark. It was only a happy day for people who had a special person in their life. Too many didn't and it depressed them. Let's have I love you day and you can give flowers to anyone, cards to anyone – and make sure you do. Reach out to those you know who live alone. This is not a suggestion. This is a commandment. It shouldn't be necessary to tell you that, but the God Center wants everything completely understood by everyone. To save humanity is to correct behavior, set up wholesome celebrations that are all inclusive globally. Unification of a splintered-up planet and presenting the inhabitants with a loving, peaceful future is what we are all about.

"We have found Earth to be a loveless planet overall. Love should rule everything you do and say. There has been such selfish, ego-centered behavior here and we know you are capable of so much more. When the people here are consumed with acquisitions, it is too easy to ignore those who have nothing.

"Respecting and honoring those that died in service or served in service is a kind remembrance. Let Memorial Day be the last Sunday of May.

"Mother's Day and Father's Day is something we know you find sentimental. Better you honor and celebrate mothers and fathers all the time, rather than on just one day. We know that some send their moms flowers on that day, but they rarely call or visit them. Whoops. You just lost your silly one day to honor your mom. Many women are left out of this holiday because they didn't have children. Let's have a Woman's Day and a Man's Day if you must. It's more inclusive, and please keep it simple.

"When we give you a makeover, it is complete. We encourage you to find creative ways to celebrate the days we gave you. We are giving you everything, right down to your lives to go forward, and a future. The future on Earth, were it allowed to continue without our intervention would be horrendous. Maybe a gratefulness day is in order, but we had hoped that you will be grateful every day!

"And Sundays now? It is a day of rest or recreation. Nobody should have to work on this day, which means everything closes so everyone does have the day off. Meet with your groups of friends for song, for sports and prayer. That is music to our ears. Yes, prayer! Were it not for millions praying, this planet would be toast."

Logan and Patti had moved inside due to a chilly wind and were cuddled up on the sofa listening to the Godcast.

"Wow, no more Christmas? That was my favorite time of year," she whined.

"Hey, we will adjust. Now that Jesus is not the reason, what's the point? Besides, it had evolved into, what did God say, a trillion-dollar waste? Think about it, honey. What did we spend on Christmas every year for the boys?"

"I know you're right Logan, but still.....I'll miss the traditions," Patti said.

"We will make new ones, traditions that make sense. I like the idea of everything closing on Sundays. Remember when we tried to have Sundays be just a family day? It was easy when the kids were little, but as they got older, they wanted to go places with their friends and not hang out with us," Logan replied."

Patti smiled at the memories. "I can't help but feel selfish and self-indulgent. I know there are so many with nothing and here we sit in a gorgeous home, with all the creature comforts. I'm so happy to see the homeless and those living in shacks all over the place are being taken care of."

"Level the playing field. Sounds so socialist and yet looking at Zytaria, I'd really love to go there, wouldn't you?" Logan said giving Patti a gentle hug. "Sounds like utopia compared to this mess of a world."

"Yeah, I would like to go there, at least for a visit. Maybe someday when we get our space technology up to speed, we can hop on over there through a portal," she said.

Logan laughed, "You've been reading the books Jessie left you it sounds like. I'm hoping to go back to NASA and see for myself what the new technology is all about. I may have to go back to school to understand it."

"Whatever it takes, Logan. I want you to be happy with your job, wherever it is," Logan gave her a kiss on the top of her head as it was resting on his shoulder.

"I'm looking at myself and my whole world with new eyes. I am becoming more aware of things I always took for granted, and I think we all did. One thing that hasn't changed, Patti, I love you more each day."

"Oh Logan, I feel the same way. You have always been my rock. Whatever comes, wherever we end up, just being together is all that matters."

We interpret it as coming from outside of us, so we want to possess love, and we reach outside for something that is already inside us.

Ram Dass
(Be Love Now)

DAY SIX

Wyatt Goodwin's home was more like a palace but many homes in Hollywood were equally ostentatious. He gathered clothes from his closet and carried them downstairs to the car in the brick paved driveway. Kathleen was packing up the contents of his drawers into suitcases. They were both getting a good workout going up and down the curved staircase that was wide enough for a car to drive up.

"Wyatt, what about your office downstairs and all the books? I can remake one of the bedrooms at my place into an office for you." Kathleen said.

"I think I'll hire movers to pack all that up and take it to your house. Maybe we can keep it in the guest house until you make room in the main house? Just moving the clothes is more of a chore than I'd anticipated," Wyatt was in good shape for his age. He did play tennis and golf regularly, but he huffed and puffed up and down those stairs carrying his clothes for an hour.

The couple intended to make the best of the new set up the God Center presented. Many in Hollywood knew they were living considerably above the "norm" and while they were spoiled in their luxury, cooperation began in earnest to share.

Marjorie Larson and her husband Brent have a home in Malibu, one of the largest, with 18 bedrooms, each with its own bathroom. It is right on the ocean, with a private beach, tennis courts and a pool. They decided to make it into a bed and breakfast eventually and would then hire another cook and more staff. They contacted the immigration officials about making room for a family to come live in their guest house, and several other families could stay temporarily until they had jobs and could move on.

A few of Wyatt's neighbors were making family compounds out of their mansions, taking in as many family members as they could tolerate living with. Others decided to give shelter and food to the immigrants temporarily until they could figure out what to do with the outrageously large estates.

The neighbors in Kathleen's neighborhood were making plans too with the supervision and suggestions of the representatives from the God Center. One home will be a new senior residence that fortunately has an elevator.

"Let's go in the family room and take a break. I contacted my sister in Kansas as you suggested. They are open to coming out and living here but want to wait and see about their job situations. It will probably take a bit of time to get everything sorted out and organized. I think the Godcast is coming on," Kathleen said.

"Good idea!" Wyatt replied, smiling at the love of his life. "We'll make it together, kiddo. I hope everyone will be as cooperative since this is certainly life changing."

"Ya know what I've just decided, Wyatt? I'm going to give away the furniture in one of my bedrooms; I mean all of it since there are so many people in need. We'll make the room your office and hire a carpenter to build shelves for your book collection."

"That would be great, honey. I'm sure there is a need for all the furnishings in my house. We'll make some calls and find homes for all our stuff. It feels weirdly good just thinking about divesting myself of stuff, like I'm going to breathe easier or something, you know what I mean?"

"I do know what you mean. I'm glad we are going through this together, Wyatt. I mean it!" Kathleen said as she gave Wyatt a hug that turned into a kissing embrace. They pulled apart when the voice of the God Center came on.

"Greetings, my children! We are happy to see the progress and cooperation on the planet. Some of the changes are making some of you uncomfortable, while others are delighted with the changes. Questions about the insurance industry have been coming from all over and here is the plan.

"No health insurance is needed. All medical will be at no cost to anyone so there is no need for health insurance. We were horrified that people could be denied surgery, artificial limbs or procedures because the insurance company would not pay for it. People died because of this. Pure insanity! That cannot ever happen again!

"There is a value in insurance for your property, should there be a fire, tornado, or a car wreck. That will continue with much more reasonable rates.

"We are creating as many jobs as we are eliminating. It won't be long until everyone is working at a job and if you are not, volunteer some place. Make your presence on the planet count for something. Contributing to the welfare of others in any way that you can is new to some of you, but important going forward.

"It has been noticed that America could use a few lessons from Japan and some Nordic countries about how you treat your seniors. These people have aged but they have aged with experience and knowledge that cries for recognition and respect. Their stories and experiences can teach younger generations, giving seniors an important reason to get up every day. Don't discount your gray-haired beings. They possess a wealth of information about life and love and the God Center wants you to use their wisdom gratefully. Include all living people with respect.

Some countries have had incredible success combining children with seniors. Again, our representatives will be helping orchestrate a mutually beneficial blending for you.

"Everyone benefits when the two groups merge. The young can learn while they have reliable 'babysitting' and this also does wonders for the elderly who tend to feel loneliness more when they are with other lonely adults. It was a pilot program but now it will be copied all over the planet. Everyone matters, remember that."

Jerry Collier is an insurance salesman. He inherited the business from his father, so you could say that insurance has been his life thus far.

"I'm glad we only sold property and car insurance!" Jerry said. "I know everything is being 'reassessed' in terms of policy costs, but I think we are going to be okay, Linda."

"I was afraid to even ask you since you've been in a horrible mood listening to the Godcasts. I'm relieved, Jerry, but I really wasn't worried," Linda said, reaching out and stroking Jerry's arm as they sat at the kitchen table watching the broadcast on his laptop. In the eleven years they have been married, they'd had one son, Scott. Linda was a fourth-grade teacher who was looking forward to the raise she was going to get.

"This has been one hell of a week, hasn't it? I've been up, I've been down. In the end, I feel this has been a good thing. Drastic, but needed, ya know what I mean?"

"Yes I do, Jerry. I'm kinda with you. But seeing all the global cleansing, I mean, seriously, you cannot NOT believe this is God. A lot of the things that are getting fixed sure needed it. You know I've been heartsick over the living conditions of some of my students, and the fact that the only meal they have is at school. Just the fact that hunger will be eliminated ought to make believers out of everyone."

"Absolutely, and I am beginning to have the belief that all that is being so drastically changed had to be. Things just couldn't go on the way they were."

"No kidding, Jerry. Let's hear the rest of the Godcast."

"Retired people have been plagued with financial concerns and health issues. It is true there is some physical deterioration with aging, but many of the present conditions we see have the potential of disappearing. With changes to allopathic medicine, made by using mostly natural medicines, many of the drug induced conditions from the side effects of their drugs will be eliminated. Many seniors will begin to feel revitalized. They will also be given more money to live on as needed.

"The God Center has received a lot of questions regarding charities. Do you realize that most of the charities funnel only 2-4% of contributions to the actual recipients? The CEO's of these 'charities' live in mansions making millions from you and your generosity. We are saving the Salvation Army, period. They will be getting millions to use, with reserves practically unlimited.

"Goodwill is so popular and widespread. It will now be run by volunteers. Items in the stores will have a $1.00 each price tag. The creator of this enterprise originally did a good thing. We like the idea, just not the fact that one man is making a screaming fortune from the people who are scraping by.

"The Habitat for Humanity is a good place to put all that stuff you inherited or don't need. Clean out those storage lockers, basements and garages. There are thousands of people, formerly homeless or immigrants in need of what you are hoarding.

"Animal rescue places are fantastic, so do whatever you can, either monetarily, volunteer, or adopt an animal.

"You will not be donating to the "Cure" for cancer. That, to us who know better, is a huge money maker but not for the cure. As we have said, cures are out there and will be made available to all who need it, but cancer will be eliminated due the cleaning up we have been doing here.

"Remember our words about thinking and your thoughts? The God Center is hearing a lot of whining, crying, and unhappiness. We want you to know and believe that the cause of your unhappiness is not the situation you are in but your thoughts about it. This planet is part of the cosmos. You think the cosmos is chaotic? No way! The very word cosmos means order. Your planet's order was out of order!"

"Right on! Yes, it sure was out of order." Jerry said. "I'm so glad we have a decent government now. Didn't you hate all the partisanship that led to fights that led to nobody doing anything?"

"OMG, yes. This Party of the People, or POP," she giggled, "God is funny sometimes!" Linda said.

"Yeah, who'd have guessed?"

The Godcast continued.

"The majority of people have an obsessive preoccupation with things, like all the stuff. Many get so twisted they identify with their things, yet on their deathbeds, these things never enter their minds. They think of relationships, people they loved, people they wished had loved them. Rarely will their enormous collections of rare 'whatever's' enter their minds. To value and care for your possessions is normal but the God Center is concerned with those who cannot find contentment with 'normal' levels of possessions but who do crazy things and spend crazy money to 'have it all'.

"There is a raging disease on this planet. It is the widespread disease of **more**. The U-Store-It businesses, 49,000 of them in the United States alone, profits 2.68 billion per year. That is a lot of money going to store 'stuff'.

What is all this stuff? You obviously do not need it if you have stored it, but the tact that this is costing you money? It is more insanity. We see many with garages full, so full you cannot park your car in your garage. What? More stuff you do not need.

"We want you to get your stuff out of there and do something with it. So your aunt's furniture, family heirlooms, are in there. Give the furniture away to the homeless who are being given places to live. You don't need it. And the hoarders? You want it all. It's a sickness really. We have never witnessed this on any other planet we have colonized. Not a one. Earth is amazing, and not necessarily in a good way. If you don't have room for this stuff you are storing, do something with it. Give it away. It will give you a wonderful feeling of lightness not to be burdened with stuff you don't need. Your preoccupation with acquisitions beyond your own needs must end. You cannot have it all – especially when you aren't even using it."

As the God Center was speaking about stuff and excesses, Logan looked around their comfortable living room. He deemed it not excessive, but then there was the basement. "Sweetie," he said to Patti, "we really need to clean the basement out. I know we've stored things there over the years to the extent of borderline hoarding."

"Oh, I know, Logan. When this broadcast is over let's go down and start pitching. But where should we put it? Just put stuff out on the curb?"

"There's a Habitat for Humanity in town. I'll see if I can borrow a truck and we can take all of it over there, what do ya think?" Logan asked.

"I'm going to hate parting with some of the stuff from the boy's childhoods, but I guess the baby crib and all that has to go. My mom's china comes to mind as well. It's okay. We may have to relocate for your job, so let's look at everything closely. If it's really worth paying someone to move it, we take it. If not, we give it away."

"Good plan, Patti. I'll go through the garage too with that in mind. The God Center is right. All of us have too much stuff. At least we weren't paying to store it like some others, but we are still hanging on to stuff we aren't using and do not need," Logan replied as the broadcast continued on.

"You know who has it all? The God Center. No human can have, be or do anything compared to the God Center. Don't try. Nobody cares that you have the rocking chair that President Kennedy sat in or the fact that you paid $150,000 for it. Such a joke, really. Millie Sawyer in Paducah, Kentucky has the exact same rocking chair. Granted it was merely inherited from her mother Mable, so it's a family heirloom and not 'presidential'. The original cost of each chair was only $125.00. See the insanity? It's the same chair but because someone famous sat in it, it becomes more valuable. Nonsense!

"Things are things. Have enough to be comfortable, have a very special thing or two, but beyond that, how necessary is it to spend money on more and more stuff. That cute little bumper sticker that says *'She who dies with the most fabric wins!'* is cute, but oh so wrong in reality. And yes, we miss nothing that goes on here on Earth, right down to your sometimes amusing little bumper stickers.

"It's the same with food. How much you need versus what you want. The human stomach is twelve inches long and the widest part is six inches. You have heard it is a good thing to eat slowly. Do you know why? It takes approximately 20 minutes for your brain to get the message that your stomach is full. Most of you chow down like you are in some stupid hot-dog eating contest. You can finish a huge plate of food in less than 20 minutes at the pace you consume. You eat too fast, you overeat and then you take antacids for your indigestion.

"Now technically your stomach can hold one quart of content if you force it to expand. You don't want your stomach to expand continually because it will expand more easily and hello weight gain, big belly, and big problems. Eating one pint of food or two cups of food is more than sufficient. One cup fills you up when you eat slowly. The super-sized portions that you think are such a good value can cause obesity and death. We do not consider that a good value.

"We've heard that Americans when visiting France or a French restaurant, grumbling that the food is great, but the portions are too small! France is not suffering with obesity rates anywhere near what the United States has. Smaller portions are not only healthier; you'll spend less on food when you eat less. Again, it is common sense.

"Take your time eating. Watch portion sizes. All medical doctors are being trained in nutrition now, a field their prior schooling glossed over. You will receive much better and truly advanced information from your medical people now. They will be supervising their over-weight patients with God Center endorsed food programs. Eliminate the word diet. It makes people feel deprived. The first thing people ask is 'What do I have to give up?' Our answer is, 'You have to give up your fat.' and super-sized plates of food. So, we won't use the word diet going forward."

Claire, Henry and their two teenagers were listening, and they knew this was about them. All four were obese.

"One pint of food is definitely not going to fill me up!" said Ricky, their son. "Have you seen the grocery store, mom? It's all fruit and vegetables!"

"I know," Claire affirmed. "Look in the fridge! We have food to eat. Introduce yourself, Ricky, to the new food program."

"This isn't funny, mom!" he shot back.

"It isn't meant to be funny. This food program will preserve your life. We may all be able to get off the meds we take when we slim down. Since we didn't control ourselves and diet on our own, it's being done for us."

Claire made a fruit salad for breakfast. She and Henry ate the fruit but the two teens started to bolt out of the kitchen to their rooms.

"You kids come back here and eat!" Claire shouted.

Reluctantly they sat back down at the kitchen table. Their forks played with the watermelon and stabbed at the grapes that slipped around the bowl resisting.

"Finish your breakfast. Then we are going to the park. We are going to walk."

Claire was relieved that the God Center was now making all the rules, providing only good food. She laughed to herself knowing she wouldn't get the blame for what was in the fridge anymore. Who will they blame now? It wouldn't be her.

Ricky groaned. "A walk? What for? When are things ever going back to normal, mom?"

"This is the new normal, Ricky. We are just beginning now with all the newness, the new government, the new medical system, all new everything. This will make our lives better. And walking? It will help us by getting in good shape physically. It's all just common sense, boys," Claire said with confidence.

"You boys will cooperate!" Henry chimed in. "Your mother is right. Well, the God Center is right. We have abused our bodies but we are going to turn over a new leaf by eating right and getting exercise."

As they finished their fruit bowls, the Godcast continued.

"We hear people crying that they do not know what to believe in without their particular religion telling them or defining for them what the 'rules' are now. We understand because in your past you may have had blind obedience to an unquestioned authority. You are now required to make a shift to your creator. Are you even listening to the God Center? People who are listening are writing it all out, almost like your new rule book for the future of humanity. It is going to be a book called Saved, and it will be the guidebook for the entire planet and future generations.

"We have spent a lot of time with your new POP government. It has been decided that in the future, every race will be equally represented in government, as well as maintaining a ratio of 50 percent women, 50 percent men. These government people have the charge of working for you the people, to make sure each state is humming along. The needs of each area will be given their due. There will be no more lumping legislation into 500-page bills to pass. Each issue is its own bill so government can move on it easily.

"You will have a president to lead the groups but with very limited powers. There is a new constitution, simple, effectively spelling out how your legislators will oversee their areas of responsibility. Now that we have removed all incentives to become a millionaire while supposedly serving your constituents, the people working in government will have pure motivations to work for the people. More legislators have been removed, including your president. We read their hearts and there was already talk of resistance, coups and other nonsense.

"This type of rebellious reaction would only happen on Earth. All of our other project planets are so in tune and in harmony with the love of the God Center in each of their hearts that rebellion would never enter their minds.

Zytaria for instance, did in the past, have a beginning like yours, as we've told you, but the messengers cleaned all that up. People came to realize they were all one, each one an expression of God. But here on Earth? We are now your last resort since you blew off the messengers.

"The God Center has no patience for that behavior going forward after what we have done for this planet. If someone is an impediment to the progress here, they are being removed for the good of the people and planet. This is being done out of love for all. Focus is on the big picture.

"We want to talk about love. Mother Teresa, another teacher speaking for the God Center said of love, *'For this purpose we have been created: to love and to be loved.'* So beautiful!

"Wayne Dyer, another speaking for us said *'I know that the very essence of my being and the way of transforming my life is love.'* What often gets in the way of love is fear. The human race here is way too advanced, not as we had hoped, but in the realm of excuses. When you allow yourselves to know that the God Center is pure love for you all, and once you really experience the renewed planet brimming with goodness you will see nothing at all to fear. You have no enemies. There is no way to make excuses for not loving yourselves, loving each other and of course, loving God. Did you ever wonder why everything in the universe is round, a circle? Because you cannot take sides on a round circle, it is one sphere. You are all one too.

"When you look at one another on your continents, you tend to see all your differences. Yes, on the outside peoples of Earth do not all look alike., but inside? You all have a heart, which is the communication center to your creator, and your spirits are all the same. What's that saying you have *'Don't judge a book by its cover'?* It is even truer with humans. You are ONE. You are ALL ONE."

Sharing increased globally. Iceland shared technology they use to provide power from natural sources. France, who'd banned plastic bottled water, has the cleanest water, with drinking fountains everywhere with clean water. You could buy bottles or cups to put the water in if you were in the cities or parks, but the containers were never plastic. They were happy to share their water renewal programs.

In a few short days, countries were sharing rather than competing. The world stage was abuzz with hope and plans for a better future. The atmosphere was changing on many levels, from the air quality to the quality of hearts and minds. The God Center took information from the Blue Zones, where people live to 100 and more, and dispensed it everywhere to inspire people.

There was so much more the God Center wanted to give the people.

"Here are a few words from Joe Dispenza, another wonderful teacher. He says *'If you focus on the known, you get the known. If you focus on the unknown, you create a possibility. The longer you can linger in that field of infinite possibilities as awareness, the more you are going to create a new experience or new possibilities in your life.'* Oh, my children, there is god-inspiration everywhere on this planet. Please start availing yourselves of the gifts you have been given!

"Closely associated to love is the quality of integrity. There is precious little of that on the planet. Integrity is about who you are and what you do.

"When you are confronted with contradictory circumstances between what you want to do and what you know is the right thing to do, having integrity makes the difference. As Oprah said, *'Real integrity is doing the right thing, knowing that nobody's going to know whether you did it or not.'*

"She gave you all much more than that quote. Books, speakers and an invitation to spirituality that most enjoyed, but the 'religious' did not. Kudos to her for being herself. The God Center watched as the 'religious' had issues with 'spirituality' as if they thought being spiritually connected to God wasn't genuine?

"The God Center is here to tell you that those having spiritual practices are truly communicating with God. We question the integrity of the religious because what they sing and say on Sunday doesn't hit the streets. We love the closeness of our spiritual practitioners, and they are a large part of why we choose to save humanity and the planet."

"Oh, I remember that," Patti told Logan. "I think it was back in the 80's or 90's. Oprah introduced Eckart Tolle and meditation, all kinds of spiritual stuff. Because it wasn't biblical, she got a lot of flak."

"Really? Well yeah, I can see that. There was no flexibility in the religious realm. Thinking outside the box or any newness at all deviated from their teachings."

"Did I ever tell you when Maryann came over a few years ago, I had an Enya CD playing and she loved it. She asked me who that was singing. When I told her she asked me where I first heard her. I told her it was on New Age radio, and she totally panicked. She said there were subliminal messages in new age stuff, and I shouldn't listen to it. She told me to turn it off or she would leave. I could not believe she was serious.

"Then she wandered over to the bookcases and of course she had zeroed in on a book I had there on witchcraft. That did it. She chastised me for reading it! I told her there is so much out there to learn about, and I was not a witch, but I wanted to learn about it anyway. But she had had it. The music playing devil crap hidden in the lyrics, and the totally church forbidden books? She left in a huff."

"Oh my God, you're kidding me, right?" Logan said, astounded.

"No, I am not kidding. She left and I haven't seen or talked to her since. I heard from another gal we played tennis with that Maryann said I was a heathen witch and she wanted everybody to know that. If that isn't a case of being scared to death of anything outside of her religion, a religion based on never ever letting anything else be, I don't know what is!" Patti exclaimed.

"Hmm, I wonder how she is handling all this change and the elimination of her religion altogether?" Logan mused.

"There are a lot of Maryann's out there, Logan. I'm sure it's been a real blow. But ya know what? We cannot worry about that. We are all going thru massive changes so they either get on board or leave. There is no organized religion on Zytaria, yet those people seemed pretty content and happy. Maybe we won't have the capability of going there during our lifetimes, but the boys might. I hope that for them, don't you?" Patti asked.

"Absolutely, honey. Let's listen now," Logan said.

"Integrity costs you nothing. When you come from a place of deep integrity, your behavior will be congruent with your heart's desire. The God Center has a question for you to contemplate. Go inside your heart and ask yourself if who you want to be is who you are. The opportunities are endless for your love and integrity to make a difference for you and others. Take some time, to talk about it, think about it.

"Most importantly, think about what gifts and talents you have that you can give away. Yes, give away! There is no blessing in attaching a monetary value to everything you do, but a true blessing when you give it away without expecting anything in return.

"If you are a good organizer, find a place to volunteer your services. There is an abundance of talented people on this planet. Consider where your place could be in this total renovation. Bring back bartering too. Share talents without making money a priority. Simple things, like you cook dinner for the person who cut your grass. This should grow into the position of first consideration since the transition period for jobs in new areas will take a bit of time. People helping people, got it?

"The most advanced civilizations in the universe operate like this all the time. We know of three planets that do not even have a monetary system like your money. Everything is done with barter and no person is hungry. Amazing, is it not? Think for a few moments of what you can give, and what you might do."

The God Center worked with educators in the schools directly. All prior curriculums were either eliminated or totally reconstituted. A huge push for trade schools ensued, training people for the many new jobs culminated by the vast changes everywhere in manufacturing. The United States will be implementing changes to put them in line with Finland, which has outranked the United States, in science, math and reading for years.

In Denmark, the student/teacher ratio was the indicator to bring their rating up four positions on the list of best education systems. Many reasons the United States was behind educationally, were addressed. Equal playing fields were indicated in many areas as a precursor to peace. It wasn't only the monetary system that was getting leveled.

After the pause given to all for the purpose of self-examination, the Godcast continued.

"Generosity is another quality to tweak a bit here. If you give something to another expecting a reward, don't. Giving from the heart should be natural. You should look forward to being able to give because we are here to tell you that giving, sharing and helping others are the basic rules of life. Everyone benefits!

"The God Center is aware that a six-day makeover of this planet has been arduous. It's been controversial and hugely difficult for you to believe and accept, even though so many of you begged for this God Center intervention. All of you everywhere have been given a renewed sense of order, fairness and opportunity to live on this masterpiece of a planet. We are so happy to give you, once again and for all time, a robust planet in which to live. Diseases you thought had no cures are remedied. Ways to stay in complete health are being given to you with totally renovated medical systems and good foods. No human being on this planet is without food, shelter and clean water. With an equal playing field, there is enough for all to share.

"You will still have law enforcement watching over you to ensure everyone's safety. We have not eliminated alcohol, but there are limits to how much a human can have. We have seen how too much alcohol has destroyed the human body, caused fatal accidents, produced marital nightmares and caused death, directly and indirectly. We have tweaked the human biology. You are now programmed to fall asleep after three drinks of any liquor. If that happens to you, in the future, you will find the taste deplorable and never drink again. You've been warned. Think about your choices.

"For the majority of people toasting champagne at a wedding, having a glass of wine with dinner or a beer at a ballgame, you will not be affected. Moderation, people. Let you not destroy yourselves anymore. The God Center has taken over. Yes, we have changed things that some will hate. The God Center wants you to consider the reasons why, and then please realize that we found changes necessary to avert personal and global disasters.

"How simple the God Center has made things! There is no reason on Earth for every human not to thrive. Simple rules and everyone has them, everyone on the planet. Call them commandments if you want to. Love one another. Be kind. Share whatever and whenever you can. Show that you have integrity, respect and patience. Do not impose your way on others, instead ask what their way is, thereby giving up the need to be right. Reach out to others, help is sometimes as easy as a phone call. Care for all animals because the One who created YOU, created them too!

"The Earth and humanity are a project of the God Center, and we are most pleased with it. Now. And all of you must now know and agree this was the best save ever! You have been relieved of debt, given cures for your illnesses, relieved of your poisoned food products, spared any nuclear issues, and provided with leadership in your governments that will work for you. Perhaps you all should make a list of what the God Center has given you, lest you ever forget. Rejoice in possibility!"

Communicating with the IRS, the God Center laid out the new design for the future, eliminating taxes for this calendar year. With the jiggling of jobs, new rules and giving people time to get their lives on track, on a good track, the IRS also needed time to reorganize according to the new rules.

Competent people were chosen by the God Center to head departments in all the social services. The bureaucracy had created such congestion that people were not being served or helped despite the need. All systems were simplified for maximum benefit to those depending on it.

"We are preparing to de-grid the planet today. We have given you not just the best for survival but the only way you ever could survive on this planet. Nobody on the planet has ever seen anything like what we have done in six days. You will be talking about this for decades! All the Godcasts are recorded so there should never be any discussions of what we meant by doing any of this.

"So many have asked us questions about space aliens. Yes, they exist, and yes, they have been around here from time to time watching you. They are not to be feared. The reason they are watching you? There have been wagers in the universe about just how long your planet and humanity on it would survive. It was June 24th, 1947, when the term 'flying saucer' entered your vocabulary, but they have been around for thousands of years. Some of the messengers were from other planets, just as some live among you now. Are you shocked? Are you amazed you didn't know? What were you expecting, little green men? You are all one. I believe I have mentioned that before.

"We tell you this not to shame you but to tell you that you are behind, universally. What is being done here by the God Center for you is meant to give you a chance to advance as other planets have. There was no other planet in the entire universe that created religions that involved themselves with power grabs of land inciting wars. No other planet that became physically and mentally ill from their food, their love of money and stuff. The order here has been out of order for centuries.

"We have been painfully clear to all of you. We saved you and the planet. It is our most fervent hope that no one becomes an impediment to future progress. We will continue to witness developments here as the implementations of new programs, policies and general demeanor evolve. Communicating with the God Center is easy, remember? There is a God Center chip in every heart.

"We have given you 'commandments' all throughout the Godcasts. There are a few we would like to emphasize.

"Killing is not allowed. Aspire always to be content. Learning/education is sacred so at least read books. Kindness and love is all there is. You are all immigrants and aliens --- so stop using those labels. If you are blessed with excesses of anything, you must share, not hoard. Reach out to others, and always treat others the way you wish to be treated. Give love and ask nothing in return. Respect all living things. And finally, the one biggie, do not judge!"

"We have answered all the pleas for peace on Earth. You have it now because we love you. There is peace on Earth. You're welcome. Don't muck it up!"

One Version Of The Last Words Of A Dying Billionaire ----- Steve Jobs

I have come to the pinnacle of success in business. In the eyes of others, my life has been the symbol of success. However, apart from work, I have little joy. Finally, my wealth is simply a fact to which I am accustomed.

At this time, lying on the hospital bed and remembering all my life, I realize that the accolades and riches of which I was once so proud, have become insignificant with my imminent death.

In the dark, when I look at green lights, of the equipment for artificial respiration and feel the buzz of their mechanical sounds, I can feel the breath of my approaching death looming over me. Only now do I understand that once you accumulate enough money for the rest of your life you have to pursue objectives that are not related to wealth. It should be something that is more important: perhaps relationships, perhaps art, perhaps a dream from younger days.

Non-stop pursuing of wealth will only turn a person into a twisted being, just like me. God gave us the senses to let us feel the love in everyone's heart, not the illusions brought about by wealth. The wealth I have won in my life I cannot bring with me. What I can bring is the memories precipitated by love. That's the true riches which will follow you, accompany you, giving you strength and light to go on. Love can travel a thousand miles. It is all in your heart and in your hands.

Material things lost can be found. But there is one thing that can never be found when it is lost – LIFE.

When a person goes into the operating room, he will realize there is one book that he has yet to finish reading – the Book of Healthy Life. Whichever stage in life we are at right now, with time, we will face the day when the curtain comes down. Treasure love for your family, love for your spouse, and love for your friends.

Treat yourself well. Cherish others.

Made in the USA
Monee, IL
06 July 2022

99150909R10115